# L♥VE HATES VIOLENCE 3

## DE'WAYNE MARIS

GOOD 2 GO PUBLISHI[

**LOVE HATES VIOLENCE 3**

Written by DE'WAYNE MARIS

Cover Design: Davida Baldwin – Odd Ball Designs

Typesetter: Mychea

ISBN: 9781947340381

Copyright © 2019 Good2Go Publishing

Published 2019  by Good2Go Publishing

7311 W. Glass Lane • Laveen, AZ 85339

www.good2gopublishing.com

https://twitter.com/good2gobooks

G2G@good2gopublishing.com

www.facebook.com/good2gopublishing

www.instagram.com/good2gopublishing

# *ACKNOWLEDGMENTS*

*To Sa'niyah, a free and loving spirit. Remember to always do you and remain as sweet as you are. Papa loves you!*

*And here's another round. Shout outs to Ralph, Virg, Martha, Daddyo, and the rest of my family. I love y'all.*

*And T.G., what up, bro? Miss you. Hope all is well.*

*And as for Jamall and James Brown from Compton. Good lookin' out, fam, on ya encouragement. Stay free so Pops can see you shine.*

*And for y'all, my readers out there, hope you will enjoy. Good lookin'.*

# L♥VE HATES VIOLENCE 3

# CHAPTER ONE

**Bang 1**
**Caught in the Act**

**A**fter Dirt and Exavier's hit on Glen Johnson, giving Exavier one under his belt before he started his bigger mission to get revenge on Jim Jim, Detective Janikaski was on the scene to help solve the case of who did it.

"Run that video again. I think we might have gotten something," Detective Janikaski said.

The detective was hunched over the plump security guard, who searched the surveillance cameras. His fat fingers pushed the buttons, making the several screens in front of him rotate to multiple scenes that took place during the time of Glen Johnson's murder. Yellow caution tape was set up around the lobby floor, blocking the entrance to the elevators and stairwells.

"Freeze right there, young man!"

The black security guard did as he was told, pressing the button to freeze the image.

"Well what do we have here?" the detective said in a tantalizing voice.

The security guard was instructed to zoom in. As he did so, the familiar face of a young boy, who was now a grown man the detective recognized from another lifetime, appeared on the screen.

"Go to the next video. The one before

this in the parking lot."

"What is it, detective? You think you got a suspect? Mr. Johnson was a good friend of mine. He did nobody no harm. I hope ya catch the bastard who did this," the security guard said as he hit the button to the surveillance screen.

The detective watched as the screens rotated from one image to the next, while the guard went on about how good of a man Glen Johnson was. Janikaski wondered if the guy knew that Johnson was tied to a ring of drug smuggling that went from LA to Sacramento. He also wondered if he had known that, if he would still have been friends with Glen Johnson.

"Look here, young lad! I don't think ya

knew this guy as well as ya think," he said, looking at the screen that was now frozen on Exavier and Dirt as they were getting out of the Range Rover in the parking lot. "Ya good friend here was involved in more than just this library shit!" he explained as he swung his hand in the air toward the small statue of Christopher Columbus on the second floor that could be seen from the lobby. "This was a hit, and ya boy must've pissed somebody off."

As the detective looked back down at the frozen screen, he knew exactly who that someone was. At least he thought he did.

"Hey, Janikaski, over here!" a uniformed officer called out.

The detective told the security guard to delete the screen as the officer got closer.

The two stepped into each other's proximity and clashed hands along with a strong embrace. Although the two worked for different agencies, and in total contrast when it came to uniforms, it was obvious that they were strong acquaintances.

"What's the crack unit doing here? This is a homicide," he joked.

Sheriff Williams was a corn-fed-looking bastard, who looked like he was on steroids. He was white, and had a shaved head and goatee aligned with a five o'clock shadow. His uniform shirt was tight, and possibly an extra small from the way it wrapped around his arms, which made his biceps bulge as if he was a bodybuilder. But he was not, since he had a muffin top around his waist area. From the stripes on his uniform, he was probably just the guy who cruised around in his squad car all day answering calls like the one he was on at the moment.

The detective and sheriff walked outside and away from the commotion that was going on. They both had arrived at different times, but they saw the body and came to the same conclusion that the murder was indeed a hit. Once they got out of earshot, they got down to real business.

"I was just looking over the video with that fat guy in there," Janikaski began. "And it looks like that Exavier kid is all grown up now."

The sheriff looked dubious for a minute. But then came to once he realized the detective was talking about Dena's son.

"Ya talking about the little black kid from Jim Jim's crew? You think Jim Jim was behind this? I can get the crew together and go hit some spots right now," the sheriff said as he reached for his radio to make the call, before the detective tapped his shoulder.

"Hold up! Let me look into something before you make ya move," he said.

"All right, but ya know that the mayor is going to get at the chief about this one. Them bastards are pretty bold to come into the Christopher Columbus Library to pull a stunt like this!"

"Fuck the mayor, bro! He'll find something good to tell the public to reassure their safety, while those found-ations continue to give him dough to feed his fat ass," Janikaski surmised.

"Your call, bro. Let me know when you want to make a move."

"Just give me a couple of days. Let me see what I can come up with, and then we can hit the streets and rattle a few cages," the detective said as he reached into his pocket for a cigarette and lighter.

He tapped the Newport on its pack after taking it out, and then put it to his mouth to light. The smoke climbed the now-dark sky as the aroma grew and irritated the sheriff's nostrils.

The sheriff moved a few steps away to get away from the annoying smell. He swatted the smoke as if it was an irritating fly.

"Man, I thought you quit those things. That shit is going to kill you," he said.

"We gotta die of something, Sheriff. I'd rather it be these here smokes or a nice piece of ass," Janikaski said as he continued to puff and blow the smoke out into the opposite direction.

"What's up with your crew?" the detective said.

He knew about the sheriff's gang. In fact, he was tied into it to a certain extent.

Sheriff Williams was the head lieutenant of the Screw-Face Boys. He picked his litter from the thousands of recruits who started off working in the county jails that looked tough and were down for whatever. On their first assignment, he would send them on various missions through the jail to see if they fit the criteria. If they passed, they were able to be branded with a special tattoo and become part of the crew.

They were known for gang banging on other agencies and other sheriffs who even thought about going against the grain. They did extortions on club owners and other businesses mainly in the Hollywood area, where they ran most of their operation. They carried the law and enforced it with the barrel of their weapons, flashing their badges to make it legal. When they wanted to, they would hit the urban cities like Compton and Watts. And that was where Detective Janikaski played his part.

He had access to all the information that would make his and the sheriff's agencies look good. When it was time to show stats to the mayor and the public and make them aware that they were doing a good job, he would simply raid a few known spots or plant murders on innocent gang members. They would then all take a photo in front of the media for the world to see that they were doing their jobs.

So it was obvious why business owners were too afraid to come forward or the head niggaz were unjustly convicted. No one would believe them anyway. With that said, Janikaski and Sheriff Williams's business ran smoothly.

"Everything's running smooth," the sheriff admitted.

"Good. I might have something more lucrative for us if you're interested."

"Sure. Let's hear it. I can always use something extra," Williams said.

"Yeah, I know, huh? The life we live."

The coroner was just arriving as they watched the van pull up. The driver got out. She was a well-figured black lady. She had a seductive stride as she walked to the back of the van, where her partner awaited with the door open and ready to pull out the bed. The detective watched as she bent over slightly to pick up something that she had dropped. The cigarette was hanging from his lips as the cherry burned. He took the cancer stick from his mouth.

"When did they start hiring coroners like that? Bro, you see the ass on that black beauty?"

But the sheriff was not interested in black beauty. He was a real "Make America Great Again" Trump supporter. So when the detective made that comment, he made the flat tire sound with his lips.

"Oh, I forgot. You skinhead pricks hate

black pussy. Assholes! You need to listen to DJ Quick, and then ya ass might have a change of heart," the detective said.

He hit the cancer stick again, and then he waved at the black lady before putting the cigarette out with his Kenneth Coles.

"I'll holla at her later," he said. "But now, back to my real partner."

The sheriff hated when he spoke like that, with the street vernacular of the hood niggaz he enjoyed putting away. It made him so hot that his skin would turn red, and the detective knew it, which was why he played with him from time to time.

He smiled at the sheriff before looking around to make sure that they were still alone.

"I think Jim Jim is still doing business, even though I told him not to."

"What makes you think that?" Williams questioned.

"The streets talk; and from what I hear, he's getting into the weed business—that dispensary shit. They're all over the place now."

"So, how much is it?" the sheriff asked, even though he already knew there was major money involved.

"About $2 million. There's a shipment coming from up north. I say we get ya team together and lay them bastards down for good. Keep the money, but turn the weed in. It'll look like we got illegal weed off the streets."

"And what about Jim Jim? He'll just start all over again," the sheriff replied.

"I think I'm going to shut him down for good too," Janikaski said as they both headed to their cars.

~ ~ ~

It was 10:00 p.m. when Detective Janikaski hit the highway. He drove alone in his unmarked car while listening to the various calls from his scanner.

"To any available cars, drive-by shooting on 45th and Avalon. One deceased."

"Any available units near Lemert Park. Man walking down the street naked. Possibly high off bath salts."

"Any units available. Drive-by on 88th

and Western. Possibly gang related."

"Any units available. Drive-by—!"

The detective became annoyed and turned off the scanner.

"Let them bastards kill themselves and pick up the bodies in the morning. Fucking pricks!" he said to himself.

He turned on the car radio to listen to some jazz as he continued north on Figueroa. He watched as the ghetto stars were out scoping the track in their muscle cars with big rims while looking for the hookers that were trying to meet their $1,000 quota before night's end.

Today was Wednesday, which was good for the prostitutes because vice night was Tuesdays and Thursdays. When they saw the unmarked car riding down the strip, they just waved at the detective and pulled up their skirts just in case he wanted a taste.

When he saw Diamond, he pulled over and rolled down the window halfway.

"What's good, Officer? How can I be of service?" she inquired.

Diamond was a red-bone with juicy lips. She was a regular for the detective; and when she was not giving him the information he needed, she was giving him head. Tonight was one of the nights that head was given.

He hit the switch to open the door as she climbed inside. She smelled of bayberry every time he saw her. She was never slutty like the rest of the chicks that he gave a hard time to up and down the strip. Besides, she was a renegade. He did not have to worry about a pimp to get in his mix, because she worked alone. It was a win-win.

"Ya ready to clock out?" he asked.

"For you, always, daddy!" she replied while reaching between his legs to grab his business. "Ya packing as always, I can see. You want me to take care of that?"

"Why, of course, sweetheart!" he answered as he softly grabbed her hand. "But not here."

The detective put the car in gear and drove off as if he had just received a call.

# CHAPTER TWO

**Bang 2**
**King Cre'ole**

The boxing gym was light for business. It was always light on this day, which is why Exavier chose a Thursday morning to train. He knew Dirt would be tagging along with him today, and he did not want him to feel uncomfortable around a bunch of muscular black men doing their thing on the punching bags while he watched. Little did he know, Dirt was not white at all.

After going a few rounds and showing his skills on the bag, Dirt finally told Exavier that he was Creo. He knew something was wrong when he first walked inside. He asked earlier where all the brothers were and saw the expression on Exavier's face when he asked.

"Don't let the smooth taste fool you. I'm more Mandingo than meets the eye," he said while taking off the gloves. "My mom blessed me with these green eyes and pale skin. But my dad is 100 percent colored, my boy."

Dirt threw a playful right hook to Exavier's chin and grabbed him by the shoulder. "Come on, homeboy, let's go get some breakfast."

As they jumped into Dirt's Range Rover, his phone rang. When he answered, he said hello and then listened. His head nodded a few times, showing that he understood, and then he hung up. When he got into the SUV, Exavier was already inside.

"Looks like a change of plans. Iron'RE wants us back at Baldwin Hills. Something about that thing we did being on the news."

Dirt was talking about Glen Johnson, the library supervisor that was heavy in the dope game. The news reported that there were no suspects as of then, but that it looked like there might have been a hit on him. Whatever the case was, Dirt was not tripping. His mission was completed once his target stopped breathing.

Once he got situated, he put the Range Rover in gear and made a right once he got to the light on 108th and Broadway. He drove down the street and passed the old mom–and-pop stores that were turned into small businesses owned by local gang members. Exavier recognized a few of the faces as they passed by. They were all hanging out while they engaged with beautiful ghetto queens parked in their cars. He was hoping to spot Midge, and he wondered what he would have done if he had.

All the buildings they were passing were owned by Jim Jim. Most were vacant or run down and depleted, which was cool because he used them for storing anything and everything illegal that had something to do with his operation. And now that Jim Jim was in prison, Midge ran everything. It was likely that Midge was not hanging out like he used to because he had an obligation to make sure that everything was running smoothly. But Exavier knew his time was coming—and soon.

Dirt continued to drive down Broadway until he reached Manchester Avenue to get onto the freeway. He was amazed at the sight he was seeing as he drove past the shops with all the ghetto activity going on. There was nothing like this in Canada, with thugs hanging out on the corners smoking marijuana and drinking alcohol out of Styrofoam cups, while entertaining fly-ass honeys through the windows of their rides. The scene that he just had witnessed reminded him of *Boyz in the*

*Hood* with Ice Cube.

Dirt loved Los Angeles. Besides going to the clubs when he first arrived, he had not been able to get it cracking like he always dreamt of doing. He became infatuated with the smog, the palm trees, and the traffic each time he watched *Fox News*. He got a kick out of the high-speed chases that he saw almost every time he watched television, and he wondered why clowns would jeopardize their lives like that, knowing damn well that they were shooting anything black. But he would always cheer as if Yasiel Puig from the LA Dodgers had just hit a home run whenever a brother got away.

He made a left on Manchester and got

onto the 110 Freeway. When he looked over at lil' Exavier, he made his observation known.

"Any chance ya boy, Midge, was somewhere in that crowd we just passed?"

Exavier turned and looked at him.

"Nah, that nigga's runnin' shit now. I know if he's taking orders from Jim Jim that he's gonna stay tucked away somewhere and only come out at night." When he looked back toward the road, Exavier made his observation known as well. "You don't miss shit, huh?"

"Look here, brah. I get paid for shit like this. I train for this shit. Eat, sleep, and wake back up for shit like this!" he said as he looked down at his Rolex. "I like you, lil' brah. You got potential. I know what dude did to you really hurts. The killin' of ya moms and the attempt on ya life in jail." He looked back at the road. "But ya know what fucks me up the most? It's the betrayal. You didn't even snitch, homeboy. Ya held ya water, and they still did that to you. You got Heath's blood runnin' through you for sho! And Heath's my boy—a real one. He taught me a lot about this game. So best believe when the time comes, I'm gonna make sure you get ya revenge."

Dirt looked in the rearview mirror to see an unmarked car following him. He noticed that the car had been following them since they got on the freeway. Every time he switched lanes, the car would do the same; yet it stayed about two or three cars behind. He passed Exavier his phone and told him to press a button and to put it on speaker. As he did, the phone started ringing and a voice answered.

"Iron'RE, I got a tail behind me in an unmarked car. Might be them boys."

"Well, you know what to do. Play it cool and detour. If he's still tagging along, stay in an open area. Is there a service station around?"

"There's one on King," Exavier replied.

"All right, get off on King Boulevard. Pull into the station and see what happens. It may be our lil' friend, the detective. Don't give him any reason," Iron'RE said.

"Got ya, Iron'RE. Coming up on King

now. We'll be at the service station in like three minutes."

"I'm sending Heath and Goldie your way now," Iron'RE informed.

"All right, bet."

Dirt exited the 100 onto Martin Luther King Boulevard and made a left. Once he crossed the underpass to the freeway, he approached the traffic light and spotted the Coliseum, home of the Trojans.

The unmarked car was now directly behind the Range Rover as Dirt made a left turn into the service station. As he pulled beside one of the vacant pumps, the unmarked car fired up its light and pulled up to the back of his bumper. As Dirt was about to get out, the officer ordered him back inside over his squad car intercom. Customers in the service station took a minute to observe the commotion that was going on with the officer and the occupants inside the expensive foreign SUV. But they quickly went back to their business after realizing that it was just another day in the city they loved so much—but could hate at the same time.

The officer sat in his car with the door open and one leg out on the ground, which sported a pair of expensive dress shoes from the Birkenstock collection. He ran the license plate to see that it was a rental from 310 Motors. When he got out of his car, he looked around while letting the lit cigarette drop from his lips. But he put it out with a couple of twists from his expensive shoe.

The detective moved at a snail's pace as he approached the vehicle, with a swagger that could only be recognized by any African American who was raised in the streets. When Dirt saw his movement, he almost laughed, but he kept his composure as the officer pulled up to his driver's side window.

"License and registration," he ordered.

He did not look inside the vehicle. Instead, he kept his eyes on the driver from the side. He already knew who the passenger was, because he had a tagged them ever since they left the boxing gym.

"What seems to be the problem, Off—

? Oh, I'm sorry, you're a detective, aren't you?" Dirt started as he reached into the glove compartment to retrieve his registration while keeping an eye on the detective and his facial expressions. He played it cool as he handed it to him, engaging in further conversation. "What's a detective doing pulling over this poor guy in a Range Rover, huh? Don't you got some homicide to crack?"

The detective grabbed the paperwork with a grin and told the driver to sit tight while he ran his name.

Once the detective got back into the squad car, he ran the name. Damion Brock. Native of Toronto, Canada. Twenty-seven years of age, Black and

Creo. Six foot two and 190 pounds. Occupation: security business for high-profile celebrities named Brock's Keep Them Safe Security.

As the detective continued to run his name, another Range Rover pulled into the service station along the back wall. Heath and Goldie parked their silver SUV facing Dirt as they both sat inconspicuously behind the tinted windows.

When Detective Janikaski came back to the window, he had his hand on his service weapon. He looked at Exavier this time.

"You playing with the big leagues, huh, boy?"

Exavier looked at him and wished he

would have followed his first instincts when they first got pulled over by jumping out and running, because he knew that Dirt was armed. He was not going to go back to jail. But when he thought about the Glen Johnson murder and the possibility of them being discovered, terror suddenly fell on his face.

The detective watched as mixed emotions traveled through Exavier's brain. He wondered if he was to arrest the both of them right now, if he would be able to get answers out of the bastards. Not that he really gave a damn about the victim. He was just another dead, black lowlife who tried to play the system with that "supervisor of a major library" bullshit. How he got that far, he had no idea, the detective thought. But his clock had been punched, so the detective did not have to worry about him any longer.

Now he had a new project: the Canadian bastard. What was he doing down here in the States? He was a young cat in an expensive Range Rover, but what business did he have with the lowlife son of a bitch, Exavier. He was about to find out, and so was Exavier, when Dirt reached for the handle of his 9mm, which sat under his right thigh.

Dirt saw when Heath and Goldie pulled in earlier and parked at the back wall dead ahead of them.

As the detective was conducting his

background check, Goldie hit the head-lights to let Dirt know that they were on point.

"What you got ya hand on ya pistol for, Detective?" Dirt asked as he gripped his just the same. "I know you ran my name and saw that I got the right to carry. So just to let you know, I got a fat 9mm sitting under my leg with one in the brain."

The detective studied Dirt for a minute. He was amused by the Canadian's sarcasm with LA's law enforcement, and he wondered if the young man knew what city he was in, let alone what country. He had a mouth on him, the detective thought. Just like all the other lowlifes that he pulled over. The only difference with them was that once they saw his weapon was drawn, they knew to shut the hell up. But Dirt just kept on and on as if he was a Moorish-American who had immunity.

As Dirt continued talking, two sheriff cars pulled up. Heath and Goldie screwed on the silencers to the MACs that were now in their laps. As the officers jumped out of their cars with guns drawn, Goldie turned the ignition on, and the Range Rover came alive.

It was a nice morning out. Customers walked and talked on their phones as they approached the doors to the service station to pay for gas and other items. The music flowed softly from the ceiling speakers, comforting customers while they spent their money.

A young Hispanic girl walked aimlessly toward the doors with her slushy drink in one hand and candy in the other, while her mother walked behind her and placed her wallet into her purse. When the little girl's mother looked up, she suddenly grabbed her daughter by the arms and pulled her away from the exit.

"Get out of the car now with your hands up!" the detective ordered with his gun fully extended and pointed at the driver's side window.

The two sheriffs locked in on Exavier in the passenger seat with their service weapons drawn.

"We better get this over with before the

cavalry comes," Goldie announced as he put the Range Rover in gear.

Dirt had his hand on his pistol, which was now sitting on his lap. He looked over at Exavier and saw the two officers with their guns aimed at the window. When he saw the silver Range Rover slowly approaching, he already knew what time it was. His left hand came out of the window as if he was going to open the door and throw out his keys.

"When I tell you to lean back, do it!" he whispered to Exavier. "Okay, Detective, as you wish. I'm coming out."

The silver Range Rover moved at a snail's pace while getting closer. As it approached, the windows fell down all the way.

"Driver, I won't tell you again. Get out of the—!"

*Poof! Poof! Poof!*

"Now!"

Exavier leaned back as the window fell down.

*Pop! Pop! Pop!*

Two bullets smashed into one of the officers on the passenger side of Dirt's Range Rover. One found its way just above his bulletproof vest, striking him in the neck. He dropped immediately.

*Pop! Pop! Pop!*

Dirt fired more rounds as he put the Range Rover in gear and pushed the accelerator.

*Poof! Poof! Poof!*

The MAC-10 spit all fifty-two rounds into Janikaski's squad car, which he used for cover. Heath reloaded as Goldie pulled the Range Rover around the back of the squad car. The second officer was face down with blood running from his head. Detective Janikaski moved around the squad car as the Range Rover circled around it. He tried to reload his weapon but could not, because Heath continued to fire.

"Let's get outta here!" Heath said as the silver Range Rover smashed its way through traffic and headed west down Martin Luther King Boulevard toward Baldwin Hills.

Heath took the weapon from Goldie's

lap as he drove, and put both of the MACs and ammo into a black gym bag.

Once they got to Vermont Avenue, Goldie pulled into the shopping center and quickly parked next to McDonald's. The two of them jumped out of the Range Rover and got into a black Challenger that was parked two cars down and smashed out.

A well-dressed white woman in her early thirties, wearing an all-black blazer suit and high heels, jumped into the silver Range Rover when she walked out of the McDonald's with her phone glued to her ear.

"I'm getting into the car now, Iron'RE. They just left," she said as she hung up and drove off.

The Challenger headed back to the scene of the crime. As it arrived, just meters away, Heath saw that the paramedics had arrived with an entourage of officers from different agencies. Heath looked at the bullet-riddled squad car as the detective sat on the trunk while being examined by the EMT. He looked unfazed but a little frustrated as he kept swatting the EMT's hand away from his head, who was attempting to remove some of the broken glass that was embedded in his scalp.

Inside the service station, the little girl was smothered by her mother to protect her, while her slushy drink and candy were all over the convenience store floor. The little girl was crying as her mother tried to console her by offering to buy her another slushy and candy.

"Let's head out, bro! I bet that will hold him for a minute!" Goldie said as he put the car in gear and headed back toward Baldwin Hills. When they got past Western Boulevard, they watched as a silver Range Rover was pulled over by squad cars with a white woman inside. They knew that she would be all right, especially when they ran her name and found out that she was the grand-daughter of the head prosecutor of Los Angeles.

"Iron'RE sure knows how to pick 'em," Heath said as they continued down the boulevard.

Once they got to Baldwin Hills, they met up with the rest of the crew. Dirt, Exavier, and Iron'RE were sitting at the kitchen table with the other kids while plotting their next move.

Iron'RE had just gotten all the information he needed concerning Jim Jim's operation and the locations of where he kept his merchandise. He knew that wherever his treasure was hidden, he would also find Midge there as well.

When they walked inside, they gave each other dab and joined them. None of them spoke about what had happened. It was like water under the bridge.

"Barbara reached out to me today,"

Iron'RE said while sliding Heath and Goldie some folders.

Inside were photos of Jim Jim and the detective before Jim Jim went to the Feds. The surveillance photos were of the two of them doing business together counting money and distributing drugs.

Heath and Goldie studied the photos. This was a totally different Janikaski from the one he had just witnessed minutes ago. The look on his face was full of terror when the two of them let off rounds from the MAC-10. He just knew the detective had to have shit himself.

But looking at these photos right now, Detective Janikaski must have thought he was a true player. In almost all of the photos, Janikaski sported an Armani suit; and with his salt-and-pepper hair slicked back and his expensive jewelry on, he blended right in.

"I can see how he had Jim Jim fooled. But I see snake all over him," Heath said.

"Heath, you might want to see this one," Goldie said as he handed him the picture of his sister's murder, with the detective at the crime scene.

Heath studied the photo for a minute. His sister's body looked at peace, although her throat had been slashed. He looked up at Exavier, who already had seen the picture and put it face down on the table.

"What else we got?"

"Those deputies that were with him

today were crooked. They're in some kind of clique that Internal Affairs and the Attorney General have been investigating," Iron'RE explained. "We shouldn't have to worry about them. But if they get in the way when we go to hit this clown, don't hesitate," he said as he looked over at Dirt. "Good job, bro. When we get home, I got something for you."

Dirt nodded his head in approval.

"I got the detective's location. After we take Jim Jim's shit down and flush out Midge, we go pay the detective a visit."

Right then, Heath remembered that he needed to make a call. He reached in his pocket and pulled out his phone.

Candy answered on the first ring, and

Heath got down to business, once they got past the special greeting: "Hey, baby girl. What's up? How ya doing?"

He told her that he needed to find Midge. When it came to business, Heath was straight up with her—uncut. He told her that Midge was the one who killed his sister and tried to kill his nephew while he was in the detention center. He also told her that Jim Jim was the one that called the shots. Heath knew once he heard that Candy was going to see Jim Jim and give him some of that ooh wee (pussy) that she must have already had a vendetta against him. Because if he was still fucking, then he must not have known that he had AIDS.

"I need to know where to find him, so I

can handle business. Could you do that for me?" he asked as he looked over at Iron'RE. "As always, I got something for you, baby girl."

"This one's on me, Heath. I got you this time," Candy responded.

"Oh!"

"Yeah. When I heard him and Turtle talking about who did that to Chub, I really stopped liking that trick!" she said as she paused for a minute. "I do need one favor from you, though."

"Anything, baby girl. What is it?"

"I'm tired of going to see Jim Jim. I done give him enough of this pussy. He should've been dead," she complained.

"Say no more!" Heath said just before

he was about to hang up. But before he did, he just had to ask: "I'm just curious, baby girl. What lines did he cross?"

"He got my baby sister strung out on that shit. She's been in a coma ever since he's been in there."

"Say no more! Say no more, baby girl! I got you!"

"Well, Midge will be at one of the shops on Broadway and Century around 10:00 at night countin' money. I know, 'cause I heard him on the phone with Jim Jim the other day. He's gonna have a duffle bag full of money to take up north."

"I know which shop you're talkin' about. Any protection gonna be with him?"

"The shop is going to be closed. But he

always has some of his goons with him," she informed him.

Heath promised her again that he would take care of what she asked for. He had a few cats inside that owed him a few favors and wouldn't mind cashing in.

Once he was done, he hung up with Candy and shared everything with the crew at the table. Revenge would be embarked upon come week's end, and Detective Janikaski, Jim Jim, and Midge would have rendered their debt.

# CHAPTER THREE

**M**idge was flying down Crenshaw Boulevard in Jim Jim's '63 Chevy Impala, hitting the switches while Nipsey Hussle's latest CD pounded from his system. It was still a nice day out for low-riding, despite the latest broadcast of deputies taking fire from unknown suspects.

Breaking news of the incident broke out on every channel as it unfolded. But too bad for the hood niggaz like Midge who only had flat-screen TVs in every room of his crib just for show. He would miss out on something as important as cop killers on the loose.

The streets were hot. But Midge paid it no mind as he let Blue Gossip do her thing while the sun bounced off her gold flakes, illuminating her wet blue paint.

He stopped at the Liquor Bank across the street from the Crenshaw Mall and laid the ass down with a flick from the switch and hopped out.

He did not worry about anyone jacking him because he knew Jim Jim put the word out that Blue Gossip belonged to him. So when Midge hit each corner and flew through every neighborhood, all the hood niggaz showed him love.

Once he walked out from the Liquor Bank, he jumped back inside, lifted the back up, and skirted out with the rag down.

"This muthafucka is hot!" he yelled to no one in particular.

~ ~ ~

Heath, Goldie, and Exavier rolled in the Challenger on quiet. All you could hear were the sounds of the glass pipes doing their thing and making bubble noises.

The Challenger headed toward Century City to link up with 310 Motors and pick up two new rides.

Goldie was thinking about his daughter and wondered how she would respond to the new look, let alone his name. He had not seen Jai since he left the country, and he missed her dearly. He knew Heath would take very good care of her. In fact, he could not see it any other way given the circumstances.

Once they got to the car lot, they would receive two S-class Benz 550s that were compliments of Iron'RE, with whom they would meet up later. Goldie would head out to Long Beach to visit his daughter after two long years.

He had no contact with her after he left. That was part of the deal. So in her mind, he was as good as dead. She had to feel that way, because any other way was killing her inside, and it took Heath to save her.

She spent most of her time helping rebuild Exavier when he first returned home. But she found out in doing so, she was actually helping herself rebuild with the family she had acquired. It worked out well. She was able to put her mixed feelings about her dad to the side and focus back on her life, which now involved her husband and his resilient nephew.

~ ~ ~

Once he got to the door, he pondered what he would say to her. The scenery reminded him of the two years that had passed, when he was at this very spot with a pistol in his hand to kill the man to whom she was now married. He had no idea that things would turn out the way that they had, but he was glad it happened. He loved Heath and Iron'RE like brothers—brothers he never had. And he vowed never to cross a line with either one of them again.

He heard footsteps approach the door when he knocked, but he did not hear an answer. He waited a minute before knocking again, and he saw that someone had looked through the peephole. He knocked again.

"Jai, it's me, Que. Open up!"

Jai was in the tub soaking in bubbles, sipping on some red wine and listening to Jhené Aiko, when she heard a knock at the door. The tub was upstairs, but the hard knocks startled her as she jumped from the bubbled water asshole naked and ran to the closet.

She slid on a pair of sweats and a

sports bra over her damp skin and pushed a few numbers on the keypad. When the back of the closet opened up, she grabbed a Desert Eagle from the collection, slipped in a clip, and ran downstairs.

As the knocks continued, she did not know what to do from there. Heath had warned her to be on point while he was gone and to call him if she needed anything. Her phone was upstairs, and she did not feel like running back to retrieve it. So she walked to the door and looked through the peephole, only to see a stranger standing there hollering that his name was Que.

Jai saw that the man was unarmed, but his attire reminded her of Heath and the guys with whom he used to hang around—nice suits and jewelry. It all reminded her of her episode when she first met Iron'RE.

"Fuck!" she said to herself as she opened the door with force and pointed the gun dead in his face. "Who the fuck are you?"

"Wait! Jai! It's me!" Que said loudly, with his hands in the air and a confused look on his face. "It's me, baby girl, Que! It's me, your father!"

At this point he had forgotten about his earlier contemplation about how she would react to the new look once he stood in front of her. It did not register until now, with the big piece of chrome steel that was aimed at his melon.

His hands continued upright as he made the suggestion of going into his suit jacket, with her permission, to retrieve his cell phone. Her hands were not shaking this time as they were when she first met Iron'RE with the .380 caliber pistol in the same position. This time she was still and calm, except for her voice. She told him to go ahead.

"But if you even fart, nigga, I'll bust your brain, homeboy!"

Goldie was proud inside when he heard her bark like that, but he was afraid to show it in fear of her actually pulling the trigger.

Once he got the phone, he pushed a button and handed it to her, knowing that the recipient of the call would answer. When Heath answered, she spoke through the phone.

"Baby, is that you?" Jai responded with brief confusion until Heath explained over the phone. "OMG, is it really him!"

The gun stayed in position, and so did Goldie's hands as she continued.

"But how? Why? When did this all take place?"

Heath assured her that Goldie was her father, and to put the gun down so that the man could come inside and tell her all about it.

Once she hung up, she did just that. She gave him a long hug as Goldie put his arms down to reciprocate. The hug was endearing, long, and emotional. Jai did not want to let go. She thought this moment would never happen again. A tear fell down her cheek as Goldie broke free from the embrace and took her by the hand to go inside.

Once they were in the house, Jai closed the door and made sure that it was locked before setting down the Desert Eagle on the kitchen counter.

Goldie looked around and admired the exquisite taste that his daughter brought to their abode. What was once a home decorated for a bachelor now showcased decor of love and warmth, with family vacation photos and accomplishments plastered on the walls.

As he sat on the leather sectional, his daughter walked back in with a refreshment, which was a shot of Hennessy on ice. She handed him his glass as she held the other one to her lips to take a sip. She studied her father for a moment with an amusing look on her face. The surgery seemed to have taken about ten years off his adult life.

He was handsome in a weird kind of way, she thought to herself. She knew that it felt weird because of the fact that this was her father.

"You look like a young version of Wesley Snipes. Is that what you wanted? Ugh!" she joked because she knew that she was a huge fan of the actor.

As she took another sip of her drink, she realized that she was still in her sports bra, so she grabbed her "Just Do It" Nike T-shirt that was hanging on the back of the bar stool and put it on.

Jai knew that they had a lot to talk about, and she wondered how long her father was staying. She knew that she could never get used to the name Goldie. The name sounded like an old pimp from the 1970s *The Mack* movies. But Que would always be her father, she thought. And she let that be known as she sat down beside him and held his hand.

"It took me a long time to get used to the fact that I would never see you again. You know that, right? Heath had to put up with a lot of my bitching at first, and a lot of late-night crying because of what had to happen. But then, once Exavier came home, things got better," she explained. "I started seeing that I wasn't the only one with problems, and I started spending time with his nephew. I found out that he had been through some stuff, more than what the average kid, let alone young and black, had to go through in today's word."

She looked up at her father as he listened to his daughter with a keen ear.

"That young man has shown me a lot though. He kind of helped me put my life into perspective. He lost his mom, and I lost my dad. But his mom is never coming back, and I have mine right here—for right now. Knowing that his mom is never coming, yet being as strong as I have seen him these past years, has inspired me."

Goldie got up from the sofa, and as he took the last sip from his glass, he set it down on the marbled table in front of him. He enjoyed his moment with his daughter, but he knew that he could not stay long with all that was going on.

"Jai," he started.

"I know you have to go," she acknowledged.

"I do have to leave," he said, not regretting at all that he had come. "But that's not what I wanted to tell you." He began as he walked around the table to her and grabbed her by the hand. "A lot of shit has gone down. And you may have to come with us to Canada after this is done. It depends how it plays out. Are you with that?"

"Hell yeah!" Jai yelled as she jumped into her father's arms. "Just say when. I don't ever want to miss the opportunity to be with you again."

It never dawned on her that Heath would be in any trouble, but she knew wherever he was, she was there as well.

"I love you, baby girl, and I always will," he told her while walking with her to the front door. "I'm glad ya doing well, sweetheart. When this is over, I'll see you again."

He gave her a long hug.

"Oh, I almost forgot, if ya point a cannon at someone, ya may want to take the safety off first."

"Dually note, Dad. I will remember. But don't scare a girl like that. I was in my vibe with some red wine while in the tub thinking about my Heath," she said.

"TMI. Kill that noise! That's y'all business," he replied in a playful gesture before he got serious. "I mean it. Safety off before ya squeeze."

"I hear you."

As Goldie opened the door, Jai grabbed the Desert Eagle and followed him. He looked out to make sure there were no cops lurking before he turned to kiss his daughter and wish her a farewell.

When he jumped into the rented Benz, he sat for a minute to reflect on the past. The memory of it all brought a tear to his face. The two long years away from his little girl were hard on him. He devoted his life to see to her well-being; and not being able to continue that, because of the circumstances, almost broke him.

He knew that he was playing it close coming back to the States, but there was nothing he would let get in his way of the opportunity of seeing her just one last time. He laughed at the officers that were gunned down hours ago, and he blamed them for his absence from his daughter for so long because of being on the run.

The sudden thought brought him out of

his reminiscence as he started up the 550 and headed to the freeway. Interstate 710 was a few miles away, which would be the connection to the 405 that would get him onto his journey back to Baldwin Hills, where Iron'RE and the kids awaited.

~ ~ ~

Midge was still finger-banging the switches when he got a call from Jim Jim to make sure that he had $2 mil in cash ready to take up north.

The glass pipes were loud, and so was the music. So he pulled over to a service station and parked in the back for privacy. Blue Gossip dropped to the ground like a majestic bitch as he turned off the ignition.

"Yeah, I'm gonna be at the shop

tonight. After I close it, me, Rock, and Tut are gonna handle business," he told Jim Jim.

He listened as Jim Jim warned him to stay on point once he arrived in Sacramento, because he was carrying a large amount of cash. It did not matter that their connect Asian Blac was saying that it was all good. He was in a cell just like he was. So trust was not an option. He also knew that if it was him on the other side of that delivery waiting on $2 million in cash while the owner of it was locked up, he was going to take that ride without a doubt. So he warned his boy to keep his eyes open.

"I got ya, bro. Tell Asian Blac to call me around one in the morning so he can let his peoples know when I'm coming. We should be out there the next morning," he suggested.

Midge listened some more as he nodded his head in agreement. Jim Jim asked about the lowrider and told him to send some more pictures, but this time with a "dime piece" in some booty shorts riding the hood.

"I got you, my boy. Listen to this shit," Midge raised the phone slightly to the air while he started up the engine and hit the switch.

Blue Gossip immediately came alive and made that famous sound from the hydraulics that would make any lowrider owner nut on himself because the ride was so hot.

"I'll hit ya up once I get to the shop."

He looked around and saw that a few rubber-necks were lurking, so he decided it was time to go.

"Let me get off the phone so I can go switch cars. A few cats just drove by lookin' crafty. They might think a nigga is broke down or something, and I ain't got the Desert Eagle on me."

He put the rider into gear as he listened to Jim Jim again.

"Okay, dually noted. Call you when I get to the shop," he said once again before hanging up.

As he pulled out into traffic, he saw two patrol cars heading in the other direction.

This time as he hit the switch, Blue Gossip was in three-wheel motion when he made a U-turn and drove in the gutter lane, passing the two patrol cars with his middle finger in the air.

I t was count time when Jim Jim pulled up the small piece of cement under which he stashed his phone. The CO would be walking by at approximately 5:30 p.m. to make sure all inmates were confined to their designated areas.

His boy, Black, was not on shift that day. Instead, CO Smitty was the one walking the tier. He knew that they did not see eye to eye, because CO Smitty believed that Jim Jim had too much juice in the prison. So the CO messed with him every chance he got, searching his cell for no apparent reason and trashing everything. He figured that it would provoke Jim Jim into assaulting him, so that he might be relocated or have charges pressed against him. But his tactics never prevailed.

Jim Jim would just smile at the CO and respond with ridiculous statements such as, "Oh well, looks like I got some cleaning to do," or "Oh wow, was there an earth-quake?"

Jim Jim refused to let the CO witness his hard-core exterior, because it would just prove his suspicions about Jim Jim and justify the CO's actions.

Jim Jim decided to have some fun today after Smitty walked down the tier and yelled, "Count time. Lights on! Stand up!"

The CO was a plump five foot seven who appeared to overeat because of his fat paycheck. He made sure to make the prisoners' time uncomfortable, even for just those five minutes it took to count the population.

So Jim Jim would turn Big Debo on him, like the neighborhood bully in the movie *Friday*. It was the scene where Stanley does not reply to Big Debo's greeting.

"What's up, Smitty?" Jim Jim yelled when the CO passed by his cell. After refusing to respond, Jim Jim would say, "Well, fuck you then, Smitty!"

Then everyone on the tier would laugh.

CO Smitty never realized that as he was trying to make their time uncomfortable, he was actually giving them an opportunity to let off some steam through laughter—and he was the laughing stock.

After the little comic relief was over, Jim Jim was ready to get back to reality. He waited thirty minutes before going through the same routine when it came to retrieving or replacing the iPhone. He would then sit back on his bunk to dial a number.

He called Asian Blac, who was in another building on the facility's yard. He told him to hit up Midge around one in the morning, and they could take it from there.

Once the cash was delivered, Blac would hook him up with his realtor to go over the locations that were already purchased by Blac so that they could go into business.

Once they were done negotiating, Jim Jim disconnected to take a minute to relax. He went onto CNN.com to watch the news that they would play over and over.

It was then he saw a familiar face, which made him immediately sit up in his bunk. He pressed the volume button on the iPhone. The detective's mug was showcased alongside the other officers who were apparently deceased, according to the teleprompt on the button of the screen.

"Deadly officer-involved shooting, and

unidentified suspects are still on the loose."

Jim Jim continued to watch as the reporter surveyed the scene with her media anchor vernacular as the cameraman zeroed in on the wounded detective being attended to by an EMT. He also noticed that the time of the incident was in the morning, and he wondered if Midge was aware of any of this. Jim Jim had to call him to inform him. He knew Janikaski like the back of his hand; and if he thought that Jim Jim had anything to do with the hit, the detective might want to retaliate.

~ ~ ~

The detective wanted to retaliate all

right. But it was not against Jim Jim. Although his plan was already in motion to hit him for that $2 million in cash tonight, the real issue was the Canadian ghost. Who was he, and why was little Exavier hanging out with this stranger? The detective hit every corner where he thought he might find Exavier to pick him up.

And if he did find him, he was certainly not going to take him to the station. He made sure to withhold any information from the investi-gating detective at the scene when he was questioned about the earlier episode. Janikaski also made sure that he would be handling this alone—with his crew of crooked ones.

**W**hen Midge arrived at the shop, he pulled into the back. His local foot soldiers were hanging out in front while saluting him with a thumbs-up as Blue Gossip returned the gesture as it danced on all sixteen switches.

"Bang that shit!" one of the goons yelled out while another one pulled the gate open for the lowrider to finally get some rest.

The sun was setting over the freeway underpass as the Goodyear Blimp flew miles away over Carson City. It was still visible as it prepared to land near Dominguez Community College.

Monster cars were peaking and preparing to terrorize the Broadway strip with their glass pipes and beefy tires, making the scene come alive all over again.

Once Midge parked Blue Gossip, he closed the gate and walked out to the front with the rest of his soldiers.

"I'm about to close shop early tonight, so get what you need out of the store: pro clubs, socks, Jordans. Whatever you're going to wear tonight, and disappear," he ordered.

"For sho, big homie!" one of his goons replied while the others followed suit.

"Yo, Tut. Check it out one time, fam!"

"What's up?" Tut replied.

"Go around back and unlock the duplex and make sure ya got the money counter set up. We got some numbers to do tonight," he said.

"For sho, baby boy," Tut said as he turned to complete the mission but suddenly had a thought. "Ya still want me to roll out with you when we done, right?"

"You, me, and Rock gonna roll two cars deep," Midge reminded him.

Tut stuck out his chin, knowing that he was about to move up in rank. Midge had some dedicated soldiers, so he knew that the loyalty was 100.

~ ~ ~

From the service station across the street, Exavier and Dirt watched as Midge pulled up into his shop surrounded by his flock of goons. The lowrider disappeared in the back as they watched the driver walk back to the front of the shop moments later. Dirt took note that there was a house in the back where he was sure they would be counting the money that night.

Candy said that Midge would only have a few people with him at the time that they would be counting the money, so he would not have to worry about anyone stealing. As they witnessed Midge pull up to the front, they knew it was almost time for business as they watched the group of goons slowly but surely start to disappear.

Once the storefront was clear of the loiterers, Dirt pulled out of the service station in the black Challenger and drove around to the back of the shop to get a visual of the whole layout. As he drove slowly past the steel bar gate, he saw the lowrider resting with two blue-nose pit bulls roaming loose on two thick pull chains.

It was a small concrete yard with one set of duplexes with solid barred windows and doors. Dirt noted everything as he observed through the Challenger's limo-tinted windows. He knew he would need some special equipment and ingredients for this mission to put the dogs to sleep. He had written down that he would have to kill the dogs with rat poison in cookie dough. Once he was done casing the location, he hit the accelerator and disappeared into traffic.

When he got a few blocks away, he pulled to the side of the street and parked in front of an old apartment complex. He waited five minutes while tapping his thumbs on the screen of his iPhone as he looked through the rearview mirror, checking to see if he had picked up a tail. When it came to his craft, Dirt was always cautious, especially in moments like this. He took every measure to make sure he was not careless and was safe, and that the mission was complete at the end of the day.

"You don't see anything suspicious, do ya?" he asked.

Exavier was sitting in the passenger

seat wondering why they were parked in front of what seemed to be a trap house. The majority of the windows were boarded up around the dilapidated complex, which sat inside the barred gate with a chain and lock wrapped around the gate's entrance used for a makeshift lock. A sign was nailed to the front of the complex that read "No Trespassing," which was obviously ignored by all the human traffic that was coming and going through the back alleyway.

Exavier watched as the fiends purchased and consumed their product of illegal substances from the side of the building, while some performed sexual favors on those who paid. As the question resonated, he suddenly realized that Dirt was not referring to the activity on the right of them; he simply saw that parking here was a way to blend in if anyone got the nerve to follow them, which was smart.

When he looked over at Dirt, he started up the car. He looked in the rearview mirror one last time before pulling away from the curb.

"Don't trip, my boy. After hanging around me for a while, you're gonna see why I do what I do."

Dirt made a U-turn in the middle of traffic and made a right once he got to the light to head to the freeway. When he got onto the on-ramp, he turned on the radio to Drake's album *Take Care* that pounded through the speakers. He looked at Exavier, who started bobbing his head to the track, obviously a fan.

"That was probably one of Midge's trap houses back there. What you think?" he asked.

Exavier knew the locations of just about all the trap houses in that vicinity, but he was not certain about that one.

"Could be that he got a bunch of them. What do you think?"

"I'm thinking that we gotta let Iron'RE know 'bout this new development just in case it is Midge's spot. If anything goes wrong tonight, and I'm quite sure that it won't, we know about that spot down the street. There could be some more of his soldiers in there."

"Makes sense," Exavier agreed.

He thought about the vision earlier of seeing Midge in that lowrider having it his way after what he had done. He had destroyed his life and taken away from him the one thing that mattered the most—his beloved mother—all for some material gain and misguided loyalty.

Once they did their thing tonight, he wanted Midge all to himself, so that he could slit his throat just like he did to Dena. He wanted revenge.

~ ~ ~

Detective Janikaski sat on an orange milk crate looking through a carved hole from the piece of wood from where he sat.

The place was a straight mess. What could have been, at one point or another, a place suitable for the average low-income recipient was now a slum. Just like most kids in urban learning institutions, furniture that was left behind was run down, abused, or depleted. Old diapers that left evidence of being worn were cast along the hallways along with the rat droppings that led to the little creatures' hideout.

Earlier that day after the attempt on his life, the detective got cleaned up and decided to link up with his crooked comrades to commandeer one of Midge's trap houses. The location was convenient for the special surveillance that he had now set up, just yards away from Midge's clothing store. It was amazing what a few badges, guns, and bulletproof vests over pale white skin can accomplish in an urban neighborhood.

For decades, the brainwash had been continuing to manipulate the minds in this inner city to fear the police. So when they came barging in with guns drawn and flashing lights, the thugs did what they had been doing for years: they ran!

It was unfortunate for Midge's crew, who were now gagged and tied up while locked in the bathroom as if they were being robbed. The crooked deputies who wore bandanas around their faces continued to sell the product through the barred door. They wore black leather gloves on their hands to cover their skin. The detective felt that the operation had to continue in case one of the fiends got the notion to inform Midge that his spot just got hit by the cops, therefore blowing his cover. So as the customers came, he continued to drop that poison into their hands.

"What you need?"

"You got a dub?" a fiend asked before he would hand cash through a hole in the screen.

The deputies passed what was just purchased through the same hole from which they collected the cash. They did the process over and over for the next twenty minutes. One deputy was amazed at how much money the trap house had just made.

"Dude, ya see this shit? There's about $3,000 in cash right here!" the deputy announced in excitement.

Once he put the bills in his pocket, he switched places with another deputy, who had been keeping watch on the goons in the bathroom.

"You're up, bro. Let's see how much you trap," he challenged.

As the term resonated, the deputy was now beginning to understand the meaning of the word *trap house*. When he sat on the empty crate next to the bathroom, he opened the door where Midge's boys were gagged and tied up.

"You bastards are some brilliant mutha-fuckas. I hope you know that. Trap house! Ya gotta be kidding me," the deputy laughed as he closed the door after kicking away a lazy mouse that ran past his boot.

At the boarded window, Detective Janikaski peeped through the hole and watched as the black Challenger lingered at the back of Midge's shop. He watched as it sat there for at least five minutes before speeding off in his direction.

As the Challenger approached the corner, the driver halted at the stop sign. That brief moment allowed the detective to identify the driver as well as the passenger as they conversed. If the detective had the capability to read lips, he would have known that the two were plotting to hit the same location. The only difference was they were going for the kill.

He called one of the deputies over to the boarded window and said, "Hey, Tip, come here for a sec!"

The deputy walked over while kicking a dirty diaper.

"What's up, J?"

"Take a look at that black Challenger at the stop sign over there. Can you see the driver?"

The deputy stooped down to one of the holes in the board and peeked through with a small pair of binoculars.

"What is it that I'm looking at here?"

"The driver. He's from Canada."

"Yeah, and?"

"That's the bastard that shot at me today and killed Mark and Cody," Janikaski explained as he continued to watch the SUV pull away from the stop sign and park right out front. "The passenger is Exavier." The deputy looked oblivious. "Don't you remember the kid that fell for the pistol he was carrying that our friend, Jim Jim, gave him? Remember, the body that Jim Jim caught?"

The deputy finally had an ah-ha look on his face when he responded.

"Yeah, I remember. The little skinny kid."

"Yeah, right! That's him!"

Tip looked again. But this time all he

saw was the passenger's limo tint.

"I had a run-in with the little kid's uncle, Heath, about a week or so ago. He's a lowlife, and did ten years for bank robbery. He now runs a bail bondsman company, and I have no idea how he did that," Janikaski said as he looked over at the deputy. "He's Dena's brother. You remember, Dena, don't you?"

"How could I forget a beauty like her? When she was alive, that was the happiest I ever saw you, J," Tip replied, unaware who had killed her—and Janikaski planned to keep it that way.

"Yeah, right! She was a pistol!" the detective replied as he looked back through the hole and saw that the

Challenger was still parked in front. "What's the chance of the uncle being tied to these two and one of the occupants of the second Range Rover at the service station earlier?" he asked.

Tip had his hand on his service weapon when he raised up. He looked at the detective, who witnessed the face of his partner turn from a pale white to a hell-born red.

The detective knew what was going through his mind. The deputy was on the verge of ripping the board from the window and sticking his .45 through the bars to clap at him like a real hood nigga.

"Not now, Tip!" Janikaski urged as he reach-ed for the deputy's shoulder. "If we go after them now, that $2 million may get jeopardized."

He knew he sounded stupid to be talking about money at that moment, after two of his men were gunned down on a call that he made off the grid. On top of that, he also knew that he would be the one to personally deliver the sad news to their wives. He wanted this operation to go smoothly, so that he could at least come to them with a peace offering.

"We need this cash, Tip. So let's stay focus-ed for right now."

He peeked through the hole again and saw that the black Challenger had pulled away from the curb and made a U-turn through traffic and disappeared.

"We'll take care of that later," he

promised Tip as he watched the activity that was going on down the street through the binoculars.

# CHAPTER SIX

*Bang 6*
*Back in Love*

**H**e had her legs over his shoulders, pounding the soft fleshy tunnel between them while she screamed at the top of her lungs. She and her best friend had a crush on Wesley Snipes ever since they saw him star in *New Jack City*.

"Nino Brown is fine as hell, girl!" is what she used to tell her homegirl over the phone when they were just teens.

And here she was some years later with Nino Brown's lookalike inside her flesh, literally making love to her like never before.

Her screams grew louder as he turned her over and entered her from behind. His long snake slipped in and out of her while he gripped her cheeks with his hand and peeled them back, making sure that she took all of him. She moved with his rhythm, grabbing his waist from behind her to give him any assistance she thought he might need. But she soon let her hands drop back down to the mattress as he pounded her even harder.

Kayla was on cloud nine right now as Goldie's head went in circles between her legs. He was serving her with his head game while she felt his familiar presence that she longed for over the past few years. The reality of Que having to leave the country at a time when her feelings for him were blossoming had left her in a state of loneliness for a minute.

It was not until her best friend, Jai, offered her a job running the club, that she was able to bounce back. But when Jai called to tell her that her dad had come to visit, just the thought of Que being back in the country got her pussy wet. The initial call was quick: "There's just one thing I gotta tell you, girl," she told Kayla before she hung up.

After they were done making love, the two lay on their backs looking up at the ceiling. The room was completely dark because of the pulled drapes, while the sounds of Jagged Edge played softly from the small speakers that were mounted in the corners. Kayla fired up a blunt and swatted the smoke as it climbed to the ceiling. She looked over at Goldie and smiled before passing him the blunt.

"Do Nino Brown smoke?" she asked play-fully.

When Goldie grabbed the blunt, he pulled from it three times and placed it in the ashtray, which sat on the nightstand next to the bed. When he reached back over, Kayla was in his arms while her head rested on his chest. She smelled of a sweet aroma that was a mixture of strawberries and cream. He kissed her on the head as they both lay there for another minute in each other's arms, silently catching the moments of their past.

"You know Jai is worried about you," she spoke up without looking at him while listening to the beat of his heart.

The rhythm was smooth and calm, just as she always knew Que to be. She thought about the last time they had made love, before he left the country. There were guns, bullets, and a bulletproof vest, all of which were strapped to his body as he calmly left the house to protect his daughter. He never told her exactly what had happened, but she knew that a life had been taken.

"Jai told me about Spider trying to kidnap her at the club," she said while looking up at him from his chest. "And she told me how you came through like Black Lightning airing shit out!"

She rested her head on his chest again as Goldie smiled in the dark. He played the scene in his head as she mentioned it, and patted himself on the back for showing up the way he did. But then he suddenly realized how all of that was tied into his betrayal to a good friend, and his smile disappeared.

"Let's talk about something else," he

suggested as he sat up on the bed.

Goldie clapped his hands in the air and the ceiling lights came on. Kayla's naked body lay on top of the covers with her nipples erect.

"Okay then!" she said. "Why the hell did you change your name to something like Goldie? What was you smoking?"

"Goldie is cool, baby. You ain't never watched *The Mack*?"

"The who?"

Goldie knew that the movie was before her time, and the basis of the name went right over her head. But he had to tease her one time because there was something about her ignorance that exposed another side of her sexiness.

"Look, Goldie was a mack who ran major game on the streets and everything in it," he began.

"Yeah, that's cool. But you are not a mack," Kayla teased him back.

The two playfully wrestled on the bed as Goldie's phallus slapped against her leg. The sight of his long piece of meat was beginning to make her hot all over again. After throwing a pillow to his face, she lay there on her back with her legs wide open with that "take me now" look on her face. He was more than happy to oblige again by grabbing her legs and throwing them over his shoulders like before, while he slowly entered her. She moaned in ecstasy and grabbed her nipples between her fingers and squeezed them as hard as she could. He looked into her eyes as he thrust into her even harder. Kayla's eyes rolled to the back of her head as she felt her toes curl. As her body began to register from the good feeling inside of her, she orgasmed while making weird, loud noises that Que had never heard before. When her vision returned, she found Que looking at her with that "who's your daddy now" expression on his face, because he knew he had just beat the pussy up.

"What's my name?" he demanded as he pulled out of her, holding himself in his hand.

Kayla smiled at him and wiped the sweat from her forehead, looking exhausted.

When she rolled over to her side to rest her head on her elbow, she responded, "Okay, Goldie. You did that. You's a mack!"

When he finished showering, Goldie

got dressed. He told Kayla that he had to take care of some business and that he would touch base with her later. There was no need to tell her the real business because whether he saw her the next day or ten years from now, Kayla always would have that love for him. She was not going anywhere.

When he finished dressing, he looked down at the bed and saw that she was sound asleep. That pussy was bomb; in fact, the best he had ever had, he thought to himself. While looking down at Kayla while she rested, he knew that she was feeling the same about him. He leaned down and softly kissed her on the lips.

"Take care of yourself, baby girl," he said as he quietly walked out the door.

~ ~ ~

As Goldie got to his car, he noticed he had received a text earlier on his phone from Iron'RE that read, "VOK."

Who ever would have known that just three simple letters would be of such great concern?

Iron'RE would always send this message whenever the kids had a mission to do, to make sure they were 100, which was another one of his codes. When they responded with the same, he knew they were all right and on their way back to his location. So when Goldie responded, he knew that it was almost time for business.

When he got into the Benz, he exited the gated community and decided to take the streets back to Iron'RE's safe house in Baldwin Hills. He rolled down Manchester Boulevard past the on-ramp to Interstate

405. The boulevard brought him through the city of Inglewood, where he raised his daughter to become the woman she was today.

The scenery brought back memories. He enjoyed seeing all the restaurants, the shopping malls, and the pedestrians walking the sidewalks with bags in hand while window shopping and deciding on what to buy next. There was a sense of calm in this city that he realized still existed. It was a city of middle-class dwellers that enjoyed the benefits of paying taxes.

As he sat at the red light, he noticed the sound of an airplane flying overhead, and he realized how close he was to LAX Airport. Goldie looked out the window of his S-Class 550 like a little kid as he watched a plane pass over him. It was right then that he realized how much he missed the city.

**W**hen he pulled up to the Baldwin Hills safe house, he parked behind Iron'RE's Range Rover and went inside.

As Goldie walked inside, everyone was gathered around the table conversing. He noticed that Heath was missing, so he inquired about his whereabouts.

Heath was in the backyard pacing back and forth along the massive landscape of sloped green grass as Goldie approached. His friend was decked out in a linen suit and Stacy Adams shoes, with his shirt unbuttoned to expose the fullness of his chest.

Heath calmly spoke on the phone while reaching out to his friend to greet him. As they embraced, he continued his conversation.

"I'm ready to cash in on that favor you owe me," he said.

On the other end Asian Blac was on his iPhone while cooking a spread of white rice with baby clams, oysters, and dried shrimp. The smoke from his hot plate climbed to the ceiling of his small cell as he fried summer sausage sautéed in garlic, curry, and Sriracha sauce, which all left a pleasant aroma in the air. This would be his meal tonight, before lying back to smoke a blunt from some of the latest flavors of kush the guard had smuggled in for him.

He listened as Heath explained to him about a problem that he knew—from where he stood—Asian Blac was able to fix. Heath knew that he would be killing two birds with one stone if Blac were to make it happen.

It had been four years since Heath last saw him. It was the day that he was released from prison. Out of all those who left before him, Heath was one of those chosen few that kept it real by sending letters and photos his first week out.

Heath knew that it was a dark place in prison. Although some cats walked around with smiles on their faces, there was always that moment where even the strong ones would break down in tears when no one was watching.

So when Heath got out, he made sure that he sent some light back inside with flicks of himself out in society enjoying life. He sent pics of being on big yachts with his new wife on the Pacific Ocean as well as the line of his expensive cars that he had stashed away in Canada in one of Iron'RE's garages. And each time Asian Blac received the love during mail call, he appreciated Heath more and more. He knew that it was hard for niggaz to keep it 100 these days.

"What ya need me to do, kin folk?" Asian Blac said as he unplugged the hot plate and put Heath on speaker.

He then placed his iPhone in its stand on top of his locker. He thought about telling Heath to hit him up on Skype so they could see each other in person, but after having a thought, he decided against it. He refused to project this inhumane vision upon his boy all over again.

"Hold up, my boy! I got ya on speaker so I can hook this food up," he said as he took the sautéed sausage from the hot plate and placed it on the lid of his bowl to cut into little slices.

He grabbed the bag of rice that cooked in a bag of scalding hot water, and then tossed the meat inside. He started to toss the bag of food back and forth from the palm of his hands like a real chef. He made sure everything blended well together.

"Now, what did the nigga do?" he asked.

Heath went into detail and told Asian Blac about Jim Jim being tied in with a detective that had his sister killed.

As Asian Blac sat back to listen, he thought about his first interaction with Jim Jim and the vibes he got from him each time they met. There was just something about that cat, he thought, that kept his antennae up. Although he was about to make a transaction that was lucrative in his favor, after hearing what Heath had to say, he would not have minded canceling Jim Jim's order.

"Working with the police, hell nah!" he said.

Blac cut open the bag of food with a razor as all kinds of thoughts were going through his mind. He then told Heath about the exchange that he and Jim Jim were supposed to make the following day, including the $2 million in cash he would receive for the multiple pounds of kush and the location for Jim Jim to set up his dispensary.

When Heath heard the news, he was surprised. He did not know that when Candy was talking about the money, and that they would be going up north for business, she was talking about Asian Blac. He suddenly started to laugh.

"Ya wanna hear something funny, Blac?"

"What's that?"

"We 'bout to hit his boys for that cash tonight. Ain't that something?"

"Yeah!" Asian Blac laughed as he damn near choked on a piece of rice and sausage that was on its way down his throat.

"But don't trip, my boy. You take care of this for me, and there's a cut in there for you, too," Heath guaranteed.

Asian Blac was stuffing food into his mouth as Heath spoke. He was not tripping on the money, because he was a three-strike felon with a life sentence and a shitload of money and properties. But who would have known that he would spend the rest of his life in a Federal prison for taking the lives of three ATF agents in a raid?

"Heath, ya know I ain't worried 'bout no crumbs," he started as he cracked open a can of soda. "That's what's wrong with these clowns in today's world. They think a cop is their friend 'cause he got ya sellin' poison to ya peoples like it's all good," he said before taking a sip from the can.

"I got you covered, bro. Consider this one on the house," he added before finishing the last of his meal. "You just do me a favor and stay out of the way. I don't want to see you come back to a place like this. You're a good nigga, my boy."

"I got ya Asian Blac. You a real one, too. Keep ya head up in there," Heath said before hanging up.

After he got off the phone, Heath looked at Goldie, who was patiently standing there while he was on the phone. He heard everything and felt bad about Heath losing his sister while he was away. He realized that during this whole ordeal, they had not had the time to really sit down with each other to catch up on past events. He never met Dena before, but he was certain Heath had mentioned her.

Heath walked over to Goldie to embrace him once again. It had been over a decade since their friendship had felt so genuine. They were like brothers; and although there was a lot of mess they had to go through the past few years, their bond seemed to be normal again.

After the embrace, Heath kept his arm around his friend as they made their way back inside. He told Goldie about Asian Blac and the money, and how Blac would take care of Jim Jim in a few days. He then looked at his Rolex before he continued.

"What's going on with you, bro? How was my wife doing when you got over there?" he asked.

"She had a Desert Eagle pointed at my head. That's how she was doing!" Goldie replied as they both laughed.

"Yeah, she's good at pointing pistols at people. Hell, you taught her that shit! You should've seen when she pulled that pistol on Iron'RE when we were lookin' for your ass!" Heath said as he continued to laugh. "I knew then that I was going to marry her!"

As they returned to the entrance of the house, Goldie grabbed Heath by the arm to stop him.

"What you think about moving back to Canada when this is over. You, Jai, and ya nephew?"

Goldie watched as Heath contemplated the proposition. He knew that this could be a good move for Exavier. After they got their revenge tonight, he knew there was nothing left for the kid except failure. That's not what he promised his sister after her request.

"I need Jai around, bro. After seeing her today, it made me realize how much I cheated her in life," Goldie admitted as he looked up toward the sky. "You know I wouldn't want her with no one other than you. Besides me, ya probably the best thing that could've happened to her. But she misses me, dawg. I seen it in her eyes."

When Heath looked at his friend, he knew how much his decision would affect his life. Goldie was sincere and anxious. Both the traits of a good father, which was something he planned on being to the children of his wife. He and Jai had made many attempts, but so far had missed the mark.

Heath pulled the handle to the sliding doors and asked, "Have you talked to Jai about this?"

"I mentioned it," Goldie replied.

"Well, let me touch base, bro. Sounds like that may be a good move, especially for Exavier."

Heath opened the door and they both walked inside.

When they joined the rest of the crew, they sat at the table where Iron'RE awaited with two shot glasses of Cîroc. After they sat down and grabbed their glasses of the Devil's drink, Iron'RE stood up to make his speech.

"All right, fam. Now that we're all here. Let's get focused on tonight's mission," he began as he looked over at Heath and Exavier. "We're down here for these two. To get revenge on these clowns for what they did to our sister." He looked over at Exavier. "And for what they did to our lil' guy here, who is now a member of our family," Dirt slapped Exavier's shoulder with a smile as Iron'RE continued. "There's $2 mil in cash inside that house that they will be counting. We're taking all of it, plus the life of anything moving."

Heath stood up from his seat, walked around the table, and whispered something into Iron'RE's ear.

"Well done, my brother," he said as Heath walked back to his seat. "All right, listen up. My boy Heath has just informed me that our friend Jim Jim will be taken care of soon as well, which means we just have to worry about Midge, who will be at the location tonight. And we'll handle the detective after we're done."

When Iron'RE was done talking, he sat down at the table and joined the others as they checked the equipment. Exavier loaded the weapons in front of him with ammunition while looking up at Iron'RE as he did the same. His dream was finally about to come true. After all these years, he was finally about to make good on his promise. Iron'RE looked up to see him watching him, and he winked at the boy to give him comfort.

# CHAPTER EIGHT

**Bang 8**
**Revenge**

"I told you I knew that bitch from somewhere. That's the bitch Candy. She got that shit homie and goes 'round knocking niggaz down with that polluted pussy she got. Bitch is like a black widow."

Big Turtle was in his garage on the phone with Midge as he told him about the word on the street. It had been two years since his brother, Chub, had disappeared. Turtle knew that it was foul play when he noticed that his little brother was not answering his phone for forty-eight hours straight. He was not in the system when he checked; and as he went by Chub's house time after time, he saw that it was unattended every time. The lowriders sat in the same position as the days before, while Rocco (the pit bull) ran around the yard unfed.

It was not until a few weeks later that he saw the footage of Chub asshole naked being ridden by a naked Candy in a ski mask as it was being live-streamed.

The careful eye of an advent reader and subscriber to the popular magazine *Smooth* spotted the unique tattoo of a black female warrior that was blasted on her lower back that she failed to cover up. When one of his boys showed Turtle the issue, he turned to the page of the centerfold. There she was, fine as ever, and squatted down with her legs wide open while looking back at the camera.

Big Turtle continued to speak to Midge on the phone.

"Yeah, I kidnapped that bitch and tied her up. It's amazing what a hot iron can do to get a bitch to start talking, just like one of those parrots from the Amazon." He nodded while listening to Midge on the other end of the phone, before he continued. "Nah, that bitch is no longer. She gave me what I needed. The bitch was dying anyway from AIDS."

Turtle paused a moment before he announced, "That was for my boy Chub."

~ ~ ~

After hanging up the phone, Midge sat
at the table to let what he had just heard
sink in. Candy was a cold broad, he
thought to himself as he fired up a blunt
and let the smoke escape his lungs as he
exhaled. He knew something was strange
about the bitch, but he also saw why Jim
Jim was infatuated with her. Candy was
like a mixture of Nicki Minaj, Blac Chyna,
and Cardi B all in one. In all of her beauty,
Candy possessed at least one attribute of
each one of those women that had all the
ballers feeling famous. But none of them
knew her secret that had each one she
slept with walking around like the walking
dead.

When Midge realized what Turtle had

just told him, he suddenly thought about Jim Jim, and he wondered if he knew he was on borrowed time. He thought about calling him to give him the update, but he decided to wait until he was done counting the money. Giving Jim Jim bad news right then would not have given him any justice, he thought, since Candy had already injected his body with the virus and was now six feet deep.

Midge made a call to Tut, who was inside the shop with the other foot soldiers. When he answered, he listened as Midge gave him orders and demands. After a few nods of his head, Tut hung up the phone. While grabbing the two duffle bags from behind the counter, Tut told the rest of the soldiers except one that it was time to leave as he locked the door behind them. He went out the back to the duplex while carrying the bags with the little foot soldier trailing behind.

Once they were inside, Tut threw the two bags onto the floor next to the kitchen table, along with two more duffle bags. This was the location where they would be counting the money while everyone else in the neighborhood was asleep.

Midge walked over to open one of the bags before he spoke.

"Everything locked in front?" he asked while locking the smoke in his lungs as he pulled from some of Whiz Khalifa KJ before blowing it to the ceiling with an exhale.

The one-bedroom duplex with a small kitchen was furnished with just a small dining set, a leather couch, and one 90-inch flat-screen television that illuminated from behind the bed sheet. The sheet was used as a curtain in the living room window, which was barred from the outside. Dayton wires wrapped in low profile tires sat in the corner with unused hydraulic pumps and speaker boxes. The interior gave the impression of a real trap house.

Tut sat on the couch as he responded to Midge's question. He grabbed the assault rifle which sat next to him, and he pulled out the clip to make sure that it was fully loaded before slapping it back in. Tut was excited to be a part of tonight's mission and to be trusted by Midge to help count the $2 million in cash.

Afterward, they would all take a drive up north, which was a dream come true for the young protégé. But this was where Midge failed tremendously. He knew he should have had some more experienced soldiers for a mission such as this one. Although it was just to count the money, anything could happen. But Midge was not thinking like that, and he would find that his decision would cost him dearly later that night.

~ ~ ~

The trap house was getting cold inside

as the night air began to creep through the cracks of the boarded windows. Although the detective and deputies had been through many raids in the past, none of them had stuck around as they had this night to witness firsthand how a real trap house operated.

Even though they did make a few thousand dollars in sales from Midge's drugs, the coldness and stale stench of the vacant apartment was beginning to get the best of them. When the detective looked at his watch, he saw that it was 1:30 a.m. It was time to move!

~ ~ ~

When they arrived at the location, Detective Janikaski parked behind the U-

Haul truck that was parked three houses down from where Midge and his crew counted the money.

Deputy Tip was relieved that it was time to leave the trap house, since he was ready to spring into action. They left the workers tied and bound inside the bathroom and thanked them for the opportunity to line their pockets with a few bills as they left.

It was quiet on the block as neighbors slept inside their homes. The street lights were on as the stray dogs ran in packs looking for trash cans to toss.

Inside one house, a pregnant woman awoke from her sleep to treat the little one in her stomach with a late-night snack. As she looked out the kitchen window, she was surprised to see four men with rifles in ski masks and vests around their chest with the word Police blasted on the front. They were running toward the duplex apartment across the street. The pregnant women immediately grabbed the half-eaten cheesecake from the fridge and retreated to her bedroom, where she was sure that she and her unborn little one would be safe from any stray bullets.

The steel gate was wrapped with a thick chain and lock that would take only a minute for the bolt cutters to go through. But first the detective knew that he had to take care of the dogs that ran up to the gate as the officers approached.

Janikaski put out his hand and called over one of the dogs by his name as the blue pit sniffed his familiar scent. The detective gave the dog a snack and scratched his head while the deputies took the bolt cutters to the chain and cut the lock. Once the gate was open, he led the dog away to join the other stray dogs as they ran down the street.

~ ~ ~

"We ain't gotta worry 'bout them mutts any longer," Heath said from the back of the U-Haul truck.

The three of them watched from the surveillance the set-up as they watched the detective jump out with the rest of his crew, strapped, while putting on vests and ski masks.

Heath was sure that Exavier and Dirt saw the same thing as they sat in the Challenger a few cars down. Heath texted the two and told them to sit tight as he watched the detective and his crew make their way through the gate.

"You think he's going for the money?" he said as Iron'RE watched the screen.

They were all camouflaged in black army fatigues and vests like the detective and his crew. They were also wearing badges hanging from their necks like jewelry from Jacobs.

"Greed is always a fool's demise," Iron'RE said as he continued to watch the screen. "These clowns are crooked. So my guess is that they're on an illegal raid, off the grid, that's probably to send a message to Jim Jim."

Iron'RE then looked at his watch.

"Our target is Midge. Let's give him five minutes and see what it sounds like. Then we go in hard!"

When Iron'RE looked at Heath, he told him to text Dirt to make sure they were on point. When Dirt texted back in the affirmative, they were all set to go.

~ ~ ~

When Janikaski put the crowbar to the barred door, he quickly popped the lock while Tip threw in the tear gas. The smoke immediately took its effect as the officers bombarded their way through with half masks and infrared lights to their targets. It happened so fast that Midge and his soldiers who were all at the table counting money had no time to react.

Nipsey Hussle banged through the speakers as they smoked from blunts when the tear gas intruded. Money flew from the tables as Tut jumped up with his rifle in hand. But he could not see because of the smoke. The music continued its sound wave as Midge grabbed his Desert Eagle and started randomly shooting. The deputy fired one round into Tut's chest, dropping him immediately. Midge continued his fire as he kneeled down beneath the table while rubbing his eyes. Tip fired two rounds, and the soldier went down beside him.

"Sheriff's Department," the officer yelled. "Stop shooting, asshole, or you're next! Put ya gun down now!"

When Midge realized that it was the police, he complied. He was still stunned as he lay on the floor next to his soldier who looked at him with a blank stare on his face. He was not breathing, so Midge knew he was dead.

Once the detective took off his mask, Midge had a dubious look on his face. He looked at the money that fell to the floor during all the action and just shook his head.

When Janikaski walked over to him, he kicked the gun from him and put him in handcuffs. He did the same to the soldier who lay next to him, while Tip did the same to Tut, who was obviously dead from the amount of blood pouring from his chest.

"What's the deal, J?" Midge asked while trying to bounce back from the smoke that irritated his eyes. "Why you comin' through hard like this foe?" he asked.

"Tip, put the cash in those duffle bags," the detective ordered. He then knelt down to Midge. "Ya boy's trying to undermine me, huh?" he said while grabbing the Desert Eagle from the floor. "I told him to close up shop for a while, and he just didn't listen."

When he raised back up, he watched

as Tip and his deputies piled the cash into the bags like he had said. Tip was smiling from ear to ear.

"Ya tell ya homeboy that his cash won't be making it up north tonight."

"How the fuck you know all that?"

The detective put his foot on his neck.

"Muthafucka, these streets answer to me. When I say talk, damn it, they speak!" Midge gritted his teeth as the boot applied its pressure while Janikaski continued to talk. "Stupid muthafucka, you got ya boys killed. Don't ya know not to shoot at the police?"

"Ya ain't the police! You're a crooked son of a bitch! When Jim Jim hears 'bout this, he's gonna put a price on ya head.

You're a dead man!"

The detective smiled while Midge threw a tantrum. He was not hearing anything he had not heard many times before, and he laughed at him while his boot was still against his head.

The door was still opened as they continued to put the money into the bags. Janikaski listened to the scanner as dispatch called for assistance to various locations—all except his. He knew he was in the clear, but he did not know for how long. He was certain the neighbors would call about gunshots in the area from local gang members, however.

"Let's make it quick with that cash so we can get up outta here," he called out.

"What we going to do with the bodies?" Tip questioned.

"As far as I'm concerned, these bastards was robbed by some neighbor-hood jackers and it all went bad," the detective answered before he took out the zip ties and put them around the arms of Midge, Tut, and the other dead body after he removed the cuffs. "What ya think?"

"I think ya wrong about one thing," the voice from the doorway said, which caught everyone off guard.

Janikaski drew his weapon, but it was too late. Fire erupted from behind Iron'RE as he stood in the doorway. His weapon was aimed at the detective, who was now ducked beneath the dining room table beside Midge, who lay with his head down as the bullets passed him by.

For a minute, Midge felt encouraged. He did not know when, but somehow Midge thought that his boys had come to his rescue.

"Kill this muthafucka, homie. He tried to jack Jim Jim," Midge yelled.

There was so much smoke and bullets flying that Midge continued to keep his head down while screaming for his boys to do their thing.

Deputy Tip returned fire as he jumped over the table while pulling it down to take cover. Money flew in the air as the table flipped over on its side.

*Poof! Poof! Poof!*

The shells from Tip's gun fired rapidly, eating through the leather couch, which stood as a barrier between them and Iron'RE and his crew.

As Goldie came from the threshold with a Mini 14 in hand, it came alive and ejected spent rounds to the floor as the slugs cartwheeled into their targets. Two of the deputies went down immediately. From the exchange of gunfire, smoke claimed the air, just as the tear gas had done earlier. The detective and Midge were cowered behind the table while Dirt, Heath, and Goldie retreated back to the threshold of the door.

Iron'RE stood in the doorway, now with his mask off, so he could witness the terror in their eyes. He had the presence of a Mandingo warrior as he held his poise with machine gun in hand. He had yet to fire a shot. And he chose not to do so, unless Janikaski did not comply with his orders. Only the detective, Deputy Tip, and Midge remained alive. The others lay dead in the corner next to the speakers, where Nipsey Hussle continued rapping his bars.

Iron'RE gave the order to release Midge into their custody, and he gave his word to let the other two go and deal with them another time. But as Iron'RE made his offer, Janikaski took it upon himself to play gangsta by raising up from the table while squeezing the trigger of the Desert Eagle and striking Goldie in the chest. Tip followed with rounds from his weapon before Heath returned fire as he yelled out Goldie's name.

*Poof! Poof! Poof!*

Once they saw that Goldie had been hit, Dirt and little Exavier followed Heath all the way as they charged at the table with full force.

*Tat! Tat! Tat! Tat! Tat!*

Smoke came from the TEC-9 as the fully clipped magazine ate through the kitchen table like termites.

When the smoke had cleared and the shooting ceased, the stench of blood and gun powder hovered throughout the small apartment's atmosphere.

Heath kicked over the table to find the

detective motionless with blood pouring from his head and torso. Tip lay on his back with his gun in hand as the huge hole above his nose revealed some of his membrane.

Dirt grabbed one of the duffle bags that lay on the floor and started filling it up with the blood-stained cash. He looked over at Goldie, who was motionless while Iron'RE attended to him, hoping that he was still alive.

When Heath looked down to the other body, he saw that he was still alive. Midge lay there between the two bodies and played dead, once he knew that the shooters were not there to rescue him. But it did not work. When Heath put the gun to the back of his head and threatened to pull the trigger, to make sure that he was dead, Midge yelled as his body trembled in fear.

"Don't kill me, bro! Take the money. There's $2 mil in cash. But please don't kill me!" he pleaded.

"Exavier!" Heath called to his nephew.

Exavier dropped the duffle bag and made his way around the table. For the first time since the shooting had occurred, he was able to see the young man who used to be his friend, but who was now his sworn enemy. He was the very one who took his mother's life and tried to take his own over a hunch. He witnessed the evil of power and money firsthand, and he promised himself that he would never let it turn him out as it did Midge.

"This bitch is still alive. What we gonna do?" Heath asked while still holding the gun to the back of the young man's head. He told Exavier to come closer, and Heath then put the gun in his hand. "This is what we came here for. This bitch right here!"

Heath kicked Midge in his face, busting his eye open with his boot. "Peel this nigga's wig back—for Dena!" he said.

Midge yelled in pain while his blood stained the carpet. He was on his back now with the pistol aimed at his face.

"Please don't do it, man. Jim Jim ordered me to do that, bro! I had no choice!" Midge pleaded for his life as Exavier moved the tip of the barrel to his forehead.

This would be his first kill. He doubted if any of his bullets had anything to do with the officers' deaths. But he knew that he had to make a decision right then that would either make or break him.

Heath started to see the tip of the barrel shake and looked into his nephew's eyes. He saw fear. He did not know whether to be happy or surprised. But he was glad his nephew had not inherited the killer instinct he had, because he knew there was something better out there for him. But he had to let him make that choice. When he held the gun for a few more minutes without pulling the trigger, Heath took the gun from his shaking hand and placed a hand on his nephew's shoulder.

"It's all right, Nephew. I got this."

When Exavier stepped to the side, Heath stuffed the pistol in a holster that was strapped to his leg and reached under his vest for the hunting knife. As he put it to Midge's face, his eyes became dilated.

"That was my sis whose throat you slit and left for dead in that hole in the wall of a motel room!"

Heath then straddled his torso and moved the knife to his throat. Fear covered the face of Midge as he flashed back to his past, and he thought about calling on a god to come save him.

"Let her see my work when you join her, so she knows I handled my business," he said as he let the blade run through his neck like a stick of butter. Blood gurgled in his throat as his eyes rolled to the back of his head. "And this is for my nephew."

Heath then took the knife, and with two stiff jabs, he rammed it into his rib cage just below his heart. Midge made a weird sound and started twitching before his heart ceased beating and he stopped breathing. Blood poured from his wounds onto the floor, soaking some of the money that was still lying there.

When Heath looked up, he noticed that Iron'RE was kneeled over Goldie while trying to revive him, to no avail. The bullet smashed into his Adam's apple and exited the back of his head as the blood drew a puddle. He was dead before he hit the floor.

Heath walked over to him and put his hands on Iron'RE's shoulder as he continued to pump his chest. Blood squirted from Goldie's throat as he applied CPR pressure to get his heart to pump again.

"Iron'RE, it's over, bro! We gots to get outta here."

Iron'RE stopped and looked at Heath. His eyes were empty. But Heath knew what he was thinking. They were all brothers and had been through shit like this many times before. But neither could imagine the outcome of one of them dying.

As Iron'RE stood up, he kept his poise

as always. He was the leader, CEO, and lieutenant, so he knew that showing weakness in front of the kids would be unacceptable.

"Dirt! Exavier! You get all the money together?" he asked.

"Yeah, Iron'RE, we straight."

Iron'RE looked at Heath and asked, "What about Midge?"

"Ya don't want to see what I did to him. Both of them are no longer—him and the detective. Now I think it's time for us to get ghost," he said as he looked at his friend for the last time.

"What about Goldie? Are we taking him with us?" Dirt said.

"Me and Heath will carry him out. You

and Exavier take the loot to the U-Haul truck and see what it looks like outside."

As Dirt and Exavier did as they were told, Iron'RE kneeled down in front of his friend as if to say goodbye. The blood soaked into the knee of his fatigues as he moved his face to close his eyes. Iron'RE knew from previous discussions that Goldie would have probably disapproved of his next move. Goldie had told him in the event of something like this ever happening to him, they should leave him behind. He had been on the run for murder for over two decades now. When the Feds had finally found him, he wanted it to be like this, so they could see he went out like a soldier. But Iron'RE had other plans.

"We're going to bring you home, brotha, to your daughter."

As Heath heard Iron'RE speak, he suddenly thought about Jai. He knew when she got the news it was going to break her.

"Besides me being her father, you're the best thing that ever happened to her," were Que's words that reverberated through Heath's mind as he looked at Que—and not Goldie, his alias. It was his road dawg, Que, he was looking at. He never went as far as calling him *Stepdad*. That was playing it close. But he let it be known at one point when Que jokingly insinuated so, with a welcoming embrace, while smiling from ear to ear. The brief reminiscence brought a smile to his face that faded as Dirt entered the doorway.

"Looks like we got some clowns driving by peepin' out the script," he said.

Iron'RE looked at Heath.

"Maybe some of Jim Jim's boys. What do you think?"

"Probably so."

Just as he said this, he heard a ringtone coming from near the table. Heath walked over to it, turned over the table riddled with bullets, and grabbed the phone from Midge's pocket. He looked at the screen and watched as a restricted call flashed across the screen. He answered it when it rang again.

Heath remained quiet when he pressed the Accept button and put the phone on speaker as he walked back over near Iron'RE.

"Playboy, how we looking?" the voice asked.

"We lookin' good, baby boy. Who dis?" Heath tried making a good Midge impression and wondered if he was successful.

"Who the fuck is this?"

Iron'RE walked over to the phone once he saw that Heath's attempt did not work.

"No difference to you who this is," he said. "Only thing that matters is that we commandeered your money and your boys are dead." Iron'RE then paused for a moment. "And guess what, Jim Jim, you're next!"

"Man, fuck whoever this is! I have some niggaz over there immediately to air some shit out!"

"You're talking about those flunky gangbangers that just arrived parked on the street?" Iron'RE asked.

"It's obvious that you got me and my organization twisted."

"Who are you then, man? And how did you get my boy's phone?"

"Man, are you stupid or what?" Heath questioned. "Ya boy is dead! I slit his throat and gutted him like a pig. And you're next, bitch!"

"Look, man! I don't know what ya talkin' about. You must got me mixed up with somebody else."

"I know exactly who you are. You like giving guns with bodies on them to little kids," Heath replied.

When Jim Jim heard that part, he suddenly realized who he was talking about. Initially, he thought that little Exavier had something to do with his life in prison; but after the smoke had cleared, he found out that his speculation was wrong.

"Look here, homie. Whoever you is, ya know how these streets is when it comes to this game."

"Ya game is boo-boo, playboy. I'm done talkin' about this bullshit. You about to see what real game is," Heath informed him as he ended the call.

Heath then put the phone to the ground and kicked Midge's dead body in the head out of frustration.

"What's the plan, Iron'RE? Do we serve these niggas or what?"

When Iron'RE walked outside, he pulled out his radio as if he was making a call for backup. He flashed the light on the parked car as he approached it. The driver started up the ignition and pulled away slowly, when he saw the police badge hanging in the center of his vest.

Iron'RE's quick thinking gave them enough time for Exavier and Dirt to back up the U-Haul truck to the gate in order to place Goldie's body inside. He saw the car's taillights from down the street as it sat at the stop sign. He did not know how much time the deception would allow him, since Jim Jim could easily make the call from prison just as he had moments ago to give his boys the green light. So he knew that he had to move fast.

They carried Goldie's body out to the truck and placed him inside and closed the hatch. Dirt pulled up alongside of them in the black Challenger, and he stepped outside with pistol in hand while the engine was still running. The taillights at the stop sign suddenly disappeared, and Iron'RE knew why, once he heard the call on the scanner of "shots fired" at their location.

"It's time! We're done here," he announced.

As he hit the back of the truck, Dirt jumped into the passenger seat as the U-Haul made its way into traffic.

As Iron'RE jumped into the passenger seat of the black Challenger, he could hear the sirens approaching. Heath put the car in gear and headed in the other direction.

~ ~ ~

It looked like an all-out war had just taken place inside the small duplex. As the police arrived and secured the perimeter with yellow caution tape, nosey neighbors—some in house slippers and bathrobes, and others fully clothed—waited behind the tape anxiously waiting to find out what had happened.

Bullet holes sprayed the walls like

graffiti in either direction. One of the detectives stuck his finger into the holes to determine the size of the caliber from which the round was spent.

"Hey, Detective, over here!" one of the officers called as he waved him over to the table that was turned on its side.

As the detective made his way over, sidestepping the bullet-riddled sofa that was also flipped on its side, he noticed the two bodies on the floor. He recognized both of them almost immediately.

The detective waved over forensics and instructed her to photograph the area before he knelt down beside his friend to place a hand over his face and close his eyes.

"My friend, what was you into?"

Detective Miller had partnered with Janikaski for a decade before transferring over to homicide. He took a liking to the Polish Stallion, as the department had nicknamed him. But that shortly changed once Miller started to witness his underhanded actions. Detective Miller was by the book and a real salute when it came to the department's motto of "To serve and protect."

The deeper Janikaski got, the more reason he saw to put in for a new partner and transfer.

He was about to make a report on someone he thought he would never have to, and he knew there would be no way to paint him as a good cop by the way the scene looked. He grabbed his handheld recorder from his suit jacket.

"We have seven victims, including three deputies and three civilians," the detective began as he looked at the seventh body. "And the seventh is one of ours. Detective Janikaski. Cause of death: a bullet shot to the head."

As the detective got to his feet, he walked over to where the deputies laid.

"Let's get some sheets in here for our brothers!" he yelled.

He looked over at the responding officers, who stood over the deputies while trying to figure out how all of this had happened.

"Was any of this on the radio?" he asked.

"Not a word. Been on the beat since 12:00 midnight, and there was no call of such until we responded to 'shots fired,'" one of the officers said.

"I thought it was just another gang shooting once I heard the call," another officer interrupted. "Ya know how these bastards are out here. For some fucked-up twisted reason, they're always dropping one another."

Detective Miller looked at all the deputies after the last officer had spoken. He had no comeback for that one; although this was not the case this time, and he was right about that. These gang members were dropping each other from corner to corner. And for what? Some bullshit fantasy that their neighborhood was better than the next!"

"Aw shit! Looks like we have Internal Affairs coming through the door. Excuse me one sec," Detective Miller said as he walked over to greet the man in his suit as he stood at the threshold with his identification visible.

"Over here, sir."

They shook hands and the detective escorted him over to the bodies to survey the crime scene. The man introduced himself once he saw Janikaski's body.

Ben was a bit overweight for his five-foot-seven frame, and he had been with

Internal Affairs for two years now. He had spent those two years building a case on the now-deceased detective and his crew of crooked deputies. So when he saw Janikaski and the three others, he was eager to close the case. But when Detective Miller saw that he was ready to conclude his investigation, he intervened.

"I'm sorry, but is that it?" Miller asked.

"There's nothing left to investigate. The detective was involved in some criminal activities, which go back to before my time with IAB. I've read all the reports," he explained as he looked over at the deputies. "The remainder of his gang is over there in the same position as he is—dead. So let's not waste the taxpayers' time and money on investigating any further."

"But look at the scene, huh? What were they here for? No drugs, and only traces of money. But where's the rest of it, huh? Tell me that something doesn't look right with this scene."

The Internal Affairs detective looked around as he spoke. Traces of $100 bills led to the doorway, some of which were soaked in blood. As he followed his instincts, it led him to a half-dried puddle of blood that was away from the other bodies.

"There was a body here. This is someone else's blood," he said as he knelt down to get a closer look.

"I know the guy that's lying next to

Janikaski. His name is Midge—a real low-life drug dealer. The department has been investigating him and his crew for a while now. Looks to me that Janikaski got wind of a large amount of money being here at the location, and he tried to come get a piece of the action. But he was in for a surprise." Ben contemplated as Miller continued to speak.

He knew Miller was a good detective who closed many homicides in the South Central area, and that he was a man of integrity.

"Now I know from looking at those holes in the walls, and from the machinery that the deputies were using, that these clowns were shooting at something big time, not to mention the Desert Eagle we found next to Midge's body. And that big time got out of here with a healthy reward."

He looked out at the streets at the tireless bystanders as they watched the coroner come in with the body bags. He then locked eyes with a pregnant women that stood on the sidewalk in boxers and a T-shirt under a bathrobe.

"Excuse me one second, Detective."

Miller made his way over to the Hispanic woman. She looked like she wanted to talk, but not in front of the spectators. Although she was a Hispanic native in the neighborhood, even she knew the consequences of being a rat. So as the detective approached, she reluctantly moved away from the crowd and held her stomach as if she was about to go into labor. Miller followed her as he moved through the crowd, excusing himself as he brushed against agitated onlookers. When he made his way to her doorsteps, she turned around.

"*Spenca*," he said. "Do you speak English?" he asked the pregnant woman in Spanish.

"A little bit," she responded in the same language.

"Can I come in, please?"

The pregnant woman looked around as if someone were to see her talking to the detective. But they were too busy observing the action across the street.

"*Si.*"

"Thank you," he replied as he made his way in through the threshold of the doorway.

The apartment was just as small as the one he had just left. But hers was much cozier. He could tell that she was very religious once he looked at the walls of religious artifacts. A picture of the Virgin Mary watched him as he sat down on the couch that was covered with a multicolored blanket.

The pregnant woman sat opposite him in a lone chair and stared out the window.

"How far along are you?" he questioned as he pointed at her stomach.

He knew that it was an awkward

question, but it was the only one that he could come up with to break the ice.

"*Ocho!*" she responded.

The detective knew that he did not want to hold her up any longer, knowing that she was this far along, so he bypassed the small talk. He attempted to get the answers he came for. He then showed her his badge.

"My name is Detective Miller and I work for East West," he said in English this time, but slow enough that the pregnant woman could understand a bit. "There was a shooting across the street tonight. Four officers were killed. Can you tell me anything about what you saw?"

The pregnant woman seemed relaxed

now as she looked again out the window.

"Four men with guns and *policia* badge." She pointed at his badge. "Like you, in moving truck. Uh, U-Haul."

The detective had his recorder out as she spoke. He recorded everything that was being said.

"Did you see their faces? The officers with the guns?" he asked.

"No, they had, uh, how you say, mask."

She then ran her open palm over her face.

"Ski mask?"

"*Si, si!*"

"The officers drove a U-Haul truck and jumped out with ski masks over their face?" he repeated.

"*Si.*"

"Ummm, interesting. Anything else you can tell me?"

"The *policia* bring out dead man, and put in the, ummm, back of the truck."

"Was he policia, too. The dead man?"

"Si," the Hispanic woman thought before continuing. "They had, how you say, big duffle bags, too."

"Note, five men dressed as cops jump out of U-Haul truck. Later come out with one dead man and duffle bags, possibly with missing cash inside."

The detective then pushed the stop button on his recorder as he stood up from the couch.

"Okay, ma'am. Thank you for your

time. You have been of good assistance."
He reached into his pocket. "Here's my
card. It has my name and number on it.
Call me if anything else comes to mind,"
he explained.

"Si, señor!"

After the detective left the house, he
watch-ed as the crowd began to dissipate.
It was 4:30 a.m. when he looked at his
watch, and he knew that the nosey
neighbors were beginning to get bored
after the bodies were hauled out. He
watched as the last body bag was placed
in the back of the van; and for some
reason, he just knew that it was Janikaski.

"Damn it, J! Was it that serious?" he
said to himself in a whisper.

After returning to the station, Detective Miller sat at his desk to go over the collected evidence. He was old school. He had joined the academy in the late '90s, but he refused to get on board with the digital age like the millennials, whose lives were spent engaging the Internet for all their answers.

Miller took notes with a pencil and pad, or recorded his information like they did on the old-school private investigator shows. He was very meticulous, which was why it took him so long to crack a case. But he was always successful in cracking his cases; and for the case in front of him now, he saw no exception.

~ ~ ~

Detective Miller collected samples from the puddle of blood with the missing body and would have it tested and sent to Ben, once the results were in. He knew that the suspects were impersonators, and he was hoping to find a match in the criminal database. This could be key evidence to crack this case, he thought, since his old partner left him nothing to work with.

After listening to his recorder for the umpteenth time, Detective Miller decided to call it a day in order to get some rest. Because as the sun was beginning to rise, he knew he would have a long day ahead of him.

"Men dressed up as cops, huh?" he said to himself while he reclined in his office chair to allow himself some shut eye.

The house was quiet this time. The duffle bags stuffed with cash were in the corner untouched as Iron'RE and the kids sat emotionless at the dining table where they all planned the takeover just hours earlier. The chair where Goldie sat was now empty, absent of his laughter and conversation, which always seemed to bring the atmosphere alive when he was present. But now, all that seemed to be alive in the house were the baby sharks that swam in the large fish tank with blue sand as they attacked the remains of a meal that was left for them at the last sun.

Exavier walked over to the tank to watch them feed. He watched as the little shark devoured what was left of the red devil fish, and he wondered if the swift black creature felt any remorse for having to feed off another's life. He thought about the episode from earlier, and all the planning and strategizing it took as well as the guns and ammunition spent. Animosity had been high, and adrenalin was built up knowing that he was about to get revenge.

But when the time came, he choked. When he got back into the truck with Dirt, only he knew that his gun was still fully loaded. He looked over at his uncle and the others who poured liquor into the glasses and raised them in the air, clacking the glasses with an unspoken toast before putting them to their lips to consume it. They were real killers, Exavier thought as he continued to watch the essence of their beings at the moment. He noted their camaraderie that they display-ed without a single word but only in action. The way that his uncle shot that gun at point-blank range mangled the face of another human being.

Exavier knew he could never be like them. He saw firsthand tonight everything that was ever spoken about his uncle's reputation, and suddenly he regretted ever pushing him to this moment.

Goldie would still be here had he not, Exavier began to think. But then he thought about his mother; and in doing so, he felt that he had to get some type of justice. Midge had to pay for how he left the woman of his life dead in that motel room. He promised her that. And tonight he made good on that promise; only he did not pull the trigger.

~ ~ ~

Summer 2015, Juvenile Detention Center

Exavier lay on his mattress looking up at the ceiling in a small cell that he had become over-familiar with during his four-year stay. His hand was in a cast once again, after breaking it from a wild punch that landed on the back of Go-Hard's head. He was fighting a beast this time. It was nothing like the last three fights in which he so savagely met victory.

Go-Hard gave him a run for his money, standing six foot one with a mixture of 220 pounds of water weight and muscle. He had a little bit of fighting skill that made even the staff excited to watch whenever he fought. But this time Exavier caught the beast off guard while using one of the stalls in the bathroom to relieve himself with a sucker punch that sent Go-Hard into the wall, leaving the piss from his dangling testicles shooting all over the place like a fire hose.

Exavier did not stop throwing punches as he continued to connect with Go-Hard's face as he tried to pull up his pants to square off. When he succeeded, he retaliated with combo after combo, dazing Exavier for a quick second with a punch to the nose that sent him back into the dorm, where all the other ward taunted and encouraged Exavier to get back into the fight.

Go-Hard was into it now. He squared off again as Exavier shook off the vicious punch. When Go-Hard came at him, Exavier planted his feet like a professional and dropped his shoulders so when he threw his next punch, it would come with all the force of his legs, gut, and arms. Hopefully, it would send his opponent to the floor. But as Go-Hard charged forward, the punch barely fazed him and gave him a chance to bear hug little Exavier, who was less than half his weight class. When Exavier bit his ear, he knew he found a weak spot, as Go-Hard released him and turned to look in the mirror. When Go-Hard had made that vital mistake, Exavier capitalized with a hard blow to the back of the head that knocked him out cold, after his head shattered the mirror with his face before hitting the floor.

The staff arrived only to see a rendition of every fight in which Exavier was involved, with the little kid pounding his victim unconscious with vicious blows that were mixed with anger and frustration. And as they picked him up to assume the position, a routine that was becoming a little redundant for the staff, they put the cuffs on the little aggressor and escorted him to the nurse's office for medical assistance. This scenario was then followed up with him being hauled off to the box.

His hand was broken in three places from the bout, and the pain was excruciating. But he felt like a boss. Exavier promised himself that he was going after every one of Midge's boys after the attempt on his life. Midge had been released before he was able to retaliate. So he was going to make them a part of his retribution by catching all of them with the element of surprise, just as his best friend had done to him.

He remembered how Midge punctured his flesh with the rusted piece of sharp metal, almost taking his life had it not been for his determination and willpower. Remembering this as he lay on the worn mattress in the cold tiny cell, he now knew that there were no rules to the game.

~ ~ ~

"Nephew! You okay over there?" The sound of Heath's voice brought him out of his reverie.

The red devil fish were no longer as he looked at the tank, while the baby sharks lounged barely exposed beneath the blue sand at the bottom.

Exavier wondered how long he had visited the past. He finally got his answer when he looked at the Rolex clock that hung on the wall like a flat-screen that showed 5:45 a.m.

The sun was only moments away from rising, bringing to light all the evil that was done in the dark. The prostitutes were making their way to the place where they would rest like vampires, while D-boys called it a wrap like the set of a bombed movie being shot. They collected their profits and closed down shop so that the kids could safely walk to school without being exposed to their illegal activities. Through the night, lives were taken from the gunshots of rival gang members to which there was an immediate response. Detectives in their suits and ties took hours to wrap up the scenes as they meticulously gathered evidence to combine with their intelligence in order to crack the cases.

Although he was certain their crime scene was still active, Exavier knew this was a case that would never be cracked. He now realized that he was in the midst of some real killers.

When Exavier walked over to his uncle and the others, he joined them for a toast. This time they raised up their glasses full of Cîroc in honor of Que as Iron'RE shared a choice of very few words.

"Today we have lost a soldier and brother. But his departure was not in vain."

Exavier watched Iron'RE continue to speak as he held his glass. He was intrigued at the solidarity between them. Yet at the same time, he felt ashamed to have been a part of something that resulted in Que's death.

"Rest in peace, Que, my brother and dear friend," Iron'RE concluded as the others chimed in.

~ ~ ~

Although tragedy struck and claimed the life of one of their truest soldiers, Heath and the others celebrated his life for the time he gave them. Que had taught Iron'RE the meaning of a true friend, as he was able to forgive him for stealing hundreds of thousands of dollars from the safe house. He also gave Heath the opportunity to find love within his DNA by marrying the love of his life. Although neither knew at the time, they all invested into each other's being each time they were in the presence of one another.

As they enjoyed each other's company, Heath observed the expression on the face of his nephew. Exavier was confused by it all. His understanding of death was that you were supposed to be sad when you lost someone you loved, like when his mother had died. It was like something had died inside of him. There was none of this drinking and toasting shit that he was seeing right now.

"You all right, Nephew?" Heath asked as he pulled Exavier over to the fish tank as he walked with him with his hand on his shoulder. "I saw the look in ya eyes when I called you over to cap Midge," he said after taking a sip from his glass. "I knew from the beginning that you didn't have it in ya, dawg. And I want you to know that there ain't no shame in that, lil' brah. Ya still a soldier at heart. And Dena would be proud of you. Not because you went on this mission, but because you made a rightful decision."

Exavier looked at him as his uncle conti-nued.

"You been though a whole lot, Nephew. Your good-for-nothing pops left you for dead for ya momma to raise you. And she could only do the best she could in that department. But ya still needed a man in ya life. And when I was in the pen for them ten years, I thought about you every day. It messed me up when she told me you got caught up with that strap," Heath said as he knocked on the fish tank and watched as the baby sharks raised at attention from the blue sand. He smiled before he went on. "I was glad I didn't have no kids out here when I left. Hell, they probably would've been going through the same shit you had to go through."

When he looked at Exavier, Heath put both hands on his shoulders as he turned to face him.

"Now, that ya my responsibility, Nephew, I won't continue to let you suffer. Tonight we gonna break this cycle of the fatherless. Although I'm just ya uncle, we gonna make life right for you from here on out. Que's death won't go in vain, brah, ya dig?"

There was a silent agreement that both Heath and Exavier acknowledged as they both stood there looking into the glass of the fish tank. They caught the reflection of the men at the table who were now playing a game of spades.

"Come on, Nephew. Let's put this night behind us," Heath suggested as he grabbed his drink to join the game."

*Text Good2Go at 31996 to receive new release updates via text message.*

*To order books, please fill out the order form below:*
*To order films please go to www.good2gofilms.com*

Name: __ _____

Address:_____

City: _____ State: _____ Zip Code: _____

Phone:_____

Email:_____

Method of Payment:      Check       VISA       MASTERCARD

Credit Card#:_ _____

Name as it appears on card: _____

Signature: _____

| Item Name | Price | Qty | Amount |
| --- | --- | --- | --- |
| 48 Hours to Die – Silk White | $14.99 | | |
| A Hustler's Dream - Ernest Morris | $14.99 | | |
| A Hustler's Dream 2 - Ernest Morris | $14.99 | | |
| A Thug's Devotion – J. L. Rose and J. M. McMillon | $14.99 | | |
| All Eyes on Tommy Gunz  – Warren Holloway | $14.99 | | |
| Black Reign – Ernest Morris | $14.99 | | |
| Bloody Mayhem Down South – Trayvon Jackson | $14.99 | | |
| Bloody Mayhem Down South 2 – Trayvon Jackson | $14.99 | | |
| Business Is Business – Silk White | $14.99 | | |
| Business Is Business 2 – Silk White | $14.99 | | |
| Business Is Business 3 – Silk White | $14.99 | | |
| Cash In Cash Out – Assa Raymond Baker | $14.99 | | |
| Cash In Cash Out 2 -  Assa Raymond Baker | $14.99 | | |
| Childhood Sweethearts – Jacob Spears | $14.99 | | |
| Childhood Sweethearts 2 – Jacob Spears | $14.99 | | |
| Childhood Sweethearts 3 - Jacob Spears | $14.99 | | |
| Childhood Sweethearts 4 - Jacob Spears | $14.99 | | |
| Connected To The Plug – Dwan Marquis Williams | $14.99 | | |
| Connected To The Plug 2 – Dwan Marquis Williams | $14.99 | | |
| Connected To The Plug 3 – Dwan Williams | $14.99 | | |
| Deadly Reunion – Ernest Morris | $14.99 | | |
| Dream's Life – Assa Raymond Baker | $14.99 | | |

| | | | |
|---|---|---|---|
| Flipping Numbers – Ernest Morris | $14.99 | | |
| Flipping Numbers 2 – Ernest Morris | $14.99 | | |
| He Loves Me, He Loves You Not - Mychea | $14.99 | | |
| He Loves Me, He Loves You Not 2 - Mychea | $14.99 | | |
| He Loves Me, He Loves You Not 3 - Mychea | $14.99 | | |
| He Loves Me, He Loves You Not 4 – Mychea | $14.99 | | |
| He Loves Me, He Loves You Not 5 – Mychea | $14.99 | | |
| Kings of the Block – Dwan Willams | $14.99 | | |
| Kings of the Block 2 – Dwan Willams | $14.99 | | |
| Lord of My Land – Jay Morrison | $14.99 | | |
| Lost and Turned Out – Ernest Morris | $14.99 | | |
| Love Hates Violence – De'Wayne Maris | $14.99 | | |
| Love Hates Violence 2 – De'Wayne Maris | $14.99 | | |
| Love Hates Violence 3 – De'Wayne Maris | $14.99 | | |
| Love Hates Violence 4 – De'Wayne Maris | $14.99 | | |
| Married To Da Streets – Silk White | $14.99 | | |
| M.E.R.C. - Make Every Rep Count Health and Fitness | $14.99 | | |
| Money Make Me Cum – Ernest Morris | $14.99 | | |
| My Besties – Asia Hill | $14.99 | | |
| My Besties 2 – Asia Hill | $14.99 | | |
| My Besties 3 – Asia Hill | $14.99 | | |
| My Besties 4 – Asia Hill | $14.99 | | |
| My Boyfriend's Wife - Mychea | $14.99 | | |
| My Boyfriend's Wife 2 – Mychea | $14.99 | | |
| My Brothers Envy – J. L. Rose | $14.99 | | |
| My Brothers Envy 2 – J. L. Rose | $14.99 | | |
| Naughty Housewives – Ernest Morris | $14.99 | | |
| Naughty Housewives 2 – Ernest Morris | $14.99 | | |
| Naughty Housewives 3 – Ernest Morris | $14.99 | | |
| Naughty Housewives 4 – Ernest Morris | $14.99 | | |
| Never Be The Same – Silk White | $14.99 | | |

| | | | |
|---|---|---|---|
| Shades of Revenge – Assa Raymond Baker | $14.99 | | |
| Slumped – Jason Brent | $14.99 | | |
| Someone's Gonna Get It – Mychea | $14.99 | | |
| Stranded – Silk White | $14.99 | | |
| Supreme & Justice – Ernest Morris | $14.99 | | |
| Supreme & Justice 2 – Ernest Morris | $14.99 | | |
| Supreme & Justice 3 – Ernest Morris | $14.99 | | |
| Tears of a Hustler - Silk White | $14.99 | | |
| Tears of a Hustler 2 - Silk White | $14.99 | | |
| Tears of a Hustler 3 - Silk White | $14.99 | | |
| Tears of a Hustler 4- Silk White | $14.99 | | |
| Tears of a Hustler 5 – Silk White | $14.99 | | |
| Tears of a Hustler 6 – Silk White | $14.99 | | |
| The Last Love Letter – Warren Holloway | $14.99 | | |
| The Last Love Letter 2 – Warren Holloway | $14.99 | | |
| The Panty Ripper - Reality Way | $14.99 | | |
| The Panty Ripper 3 – Reality Way | $14.99 | | |
| The Solution – Jay Morrison | $14.99 | | |
| The Teflon Queen – Silk White | $14.99 | | |
| The Teflon Queen 2 – Silk White | $14.99 | | |
| The Teflon Queen 3 – Silk White | $14.99 | | |
| The Teflon Queen 4 – Silk White | $14.99 | | |
| The Teflon Queen 5 – Silk White | $14.99 | | |
| The Teflon Queen 6 - Silk White | $14.99 | | |
| The Vacation – Silk White | $14.99 | | |
| Tied To A Boss - J.L. Rose | $14.99 | | |
| Tied To A Boss 2 - J.L. Rose | $14.99 | | |
| Tied To A Boss 3 - J.L. Rose | $14.99 | | |
| Tied To A Boss 4 - J.L. Rose | $14.99 | | |
| Tied To A Boss 5 - J.L. Rose | $14.99 | | |
| Time Is Money - Silk White | $14.99 | | |

| | | | |
|---|---|---|---|
| Tomorrow's Not Promised – Robert Torres | $14.99 | | |
| Tomorrow's Not Promised 2 – Robert Torres | $14.99 | | |
| Two Mask One Heart – Jacob Spears and Trayvon Jackson | $14.99 | | |
| Two Mask One Heart 2 – Jacob Spears and Trayvon Jackson | $14.99 | | |
| Two Mask One Heart 3 – Jacob Spears and Trayvon Jackson | $14.99 | | |
| Wrong Place Wrong Time – Silk White | $14.99 | | |
| Young Goonz – Reality Way | $14.99 | | |
| | | | |
| Subtotal: | | | |
| Tax: | | | |
| Shipping (Free) U.S. Media Mail: | | | |
| Total: | | | |

**Make Checks Payable To:**
**Good2Go Publishing**
**7311 W Glass Lane,**
**Laveen, AZ 85339**

CPSIA information can be obtained
at www.ICGtesting.com
Printed in the USA
LVHW041608300519
619610LV00013B/489/P